A Father’s Pride

Written by Matthew Payne

Cover Design: Rachael Edwards

ISBN-10: 1492806064
ISBN-13: 978-1492806066

DEDICATION

This book is dedicated to the Dark Lioness of Marlothi,
whose tragic tale inspired me to write this story.

ACKNOWLEDGEMENTS

I would like to acknowledge a few individuals who inspired me to write this book. To begin with, the main motivation to write this book came from reading those written by the environmentalist and independent wildlife researcher, Gareth Patterson, who has worked tirelessly for more than 25 years for the greater protection of African wildlife.

I would also like to highlight the incredible work done by both Pieter Kat and Chris Macsween from the lion conservation charity, LionAid. Their tireless campaigning to try and save our dwindling lion populations in Africa and Asia encouraged me to finish my book. My fascination with white lions was inspired by the excellent books written by both Chris McBride and Linda Tucker.

Finally, I would like to thank my wife, Rachael, for her constant encouragement and support. Without her, I could not have written this book.

CHAPTER ONE

William was born in the remote district of Anga, located in eastern South Africa. Founded by ancient African tribesmen, the name 'Anga' was said to represent the ever-changing weather of the area. In times gone by, many people in Anga had found work as farmers. Their trade was supported by the main river which meandered through the area, leaving fields fertile enough for people to earn a basic living.

In recent years, fewer rainy seasons had caused the water levels to retreat and so the land had become less forgiving. The more people depended on the river, the more it seemed to drain mercilessly away. The people of Anga prayed desperately at night for help from their Gods, but their hopes seemed to fade over time and the people eventually resigned themselves to a future away from farming. Families travelled great distances to find work, many remained unemployed and their desperation often led them to crime. Many of the younger residents in Anga had started to join poaching groups in neighbouring districts. It seemed that, along with the water, the ancient spirit of Anga was draining away.

Through the centre of Anga ran a seemingly endless track. Its dusty lay-byes were home to a number of colourful stalls, decorated with an array of vibrant fabrics, enticing fruits, ornately decorated pottery and anything else the people of Anga could squeeze a profit out of. Frantic market traders would vehemently guard their stalls, relentlessly trying to sell their stock to any passer-by within shouting range. The track itself was littered with pot-holes, making a very bumpy journey for any motorists travelling along it. Cyclists would weave from left to right to avoid the biggest of the holes and passing vehicles left plumes of dust in their wake. Further up the track and into the outskirts of Anga, another unforgiving track veered off towards Anga Farm.

The farm was run by William's father. It had survived the drying up of the river and was seen as a beacon of hope for the few remaining farmers in the area. Striking and heavily built, William's father was a quiet, hard-working man. He had a tall frame which, together with his long, strawberry blonde hair and thick beard, could often intimidate people when meeting him for the first time.

William's mother, Margaret, had died giving birth to William, so William's father had raised his son all by himself. When William was very young, William's father would often sit on the edge of his son's bed, recounting a past life of love and ambition shared with William's mother. As his father retold such stories, William would close his eyes, imagining what his mother's smile, laugh and embrace might have been like. Over the years, these tales of joy became less frequent and William and his father would seldom talk about Margaret.

Ever since William could remember, his father had encouraged him to help around the farm whenever, and however, he could. By the age of seven, William was already changing the water for some of the animals, helping to clean their enclosures and preparing their meals. William loved the array of smells that filled the air when he handled the food. However, it was the smell of the bush which really captured William's imagination. The smell would sail in from the north and, whilst closing his eyes, William would raise his head to the sky and blissfully fill his lungs with a deep breath. William loved these rare moments of complete contentment.

In William's early years, William's father had kept his son with him at all times on the farm. Most young boys would probably have felt suffocated by this, wishing for some independence. Not William. He was different to most young boys. He loved spending time with his father. With glee, William would sit on his father's lap as they manoeuvred the rusty old tractor around the farm. On the many occasions when the tractor would not start, William would try to help his father bring the machine back to life, often getting in the way much to his father's frustration. When it was time to trim the grass around the farm, William would try to help by using a pair of blunt kitchen scissors! In the early years of William's life, the pair were inseparable. However, this was not purely down to the bond between them. It was also because Anga Farm could be a very dangerous place at times. As his father tucked William into bed or made him his dinner, he would often warn William: "Listen, if I lose sight of you, something else on the farm might get sight of you so stay close to me."

Over the years, as William's father became more distracted by his duties on the farm, the special moments between the two became rarer and rarer. The smiles and laughter soon faded away and, as William grew older and more capable around the farm, he soon found himself carrying out chores without his father's scrupulous supervision. William's father sought moments of solitude rather than spending time with his son. Whether it was sitting at the kitchen table, clutching a bottle of something William could not pronounce the name of, or listening to old vinyl records in the sitting room, William's father was slowly becoming more and more detached from his son. At the end of a hard day's labour, music would blast out around the farm and William would sit all alone in his bedroom, reading a book or simply day-dreaming. On other occasions, his father would seek solitude elsewhere, leaving the farm for an entire morning or afternoon without an explanation as to where he was going.

"I'm seeing a man about a dog, is that alright with you?" William's father would often explain when William asked where his father was going. On such days, after he had completed his chores, William would wait expectantly at the top of the long track leading to the farm, awaiting his father's return. William would stare hopefully into the distance, watching the trees sway in the gusting wind. He would pull up handfuls of grass then throw them into the breeze, checking the horizon each time to look for his father's vehicle. William did not know why he enjoyed playing with grass so much, but he did! Somehow it always reduced his boredom levels.

Sometimes, William would wait for hours before his father's truck would finally come clambering up the drive. As William watched the truck bounce its way up to the house, he would have visions of running up to his father and embracing him like he used to, telling him that he loved him and that he missed the time they used to spend together. But, as the truck door would swing open and his father stepped out, butterflies always swarmed around William's stomach and he would suddenly feel awkward. Without acknowledging his son's presence, William's father would often mutter, "Are you planning on doing any work today?" William would reluctantly pull himself to his feet, pat the thick dust off his knees and carry on with life at Anga Farm.

CHAPTER TWO

"Time to get up!" William's father shouted as he opened his son's bedroom door, fumbling for the light switch on the wall. Flicking it on, he woke the now ten year old William from a deep sleep. Half awake, William stomped around his bedroom searching for his work overalls. He would often dream that one day he might spend this time looking for his school uniform, rather than a ripped pair of dungarees. Every year, his father would promise to think about letting William attend the local school on the outskirts of Anga. However, every year, William's father would dash his son's hopes by declaring that his help was still needed around the farm and that perhaps next year might be better. "Do you want food on the table?" he would respond when William would bravely question his father's decision. This, William recognised, was his father's command to let the subject drop.

After a slice of toast and a gulp of water, William pulled his worn boots on, tied his shoelaces and strode purposefully out of the back door of the farmhouse. Standing on the porch steps at the rear of the house, William thought of the neighbouring farm, over ten kilometres away, where he imagined the farmer's son striding out of their farmhouse door. Perhaps they would be greeted by the groaning of an ageing cow, the snoring of an overweight pig or the bleating from a herd of cheery goats.

As William stepped down from the porch, he was faced with an array of different sounds. Instead of the groaning of an ageing cow, a lion's rumbling growl echoed through the air. Instead of an overweight pig snoring, William heard the threatening snort from a belligerent black rhino. Instead of the bleating from a herd of cheery goats, hyenas were breaking out into shrieks of laughter. Anga Farm was unlike most other farms. It was a maze of the continent's most iconic wildlife, from the leaping antelope to the tawny lions, all of whom had spent most, or all, of their days on this earth behind steel bars.

As William jumped off the porch's final step, he surveyed the open courtyard before him. It was a relatively large, open space with a carpet of patchy brown grass. The grass was kept to the shortest length possible in order to allow vehicles a safe passage in and out of the farm through a single gate which stood to William's left. This solitary gate was the only access point in and out of the farm. William's father had decided to have only one access point many years ago as a safety precaution that would enable him to easily spot anyone trying to get in and out of the farm. It would also limit the exit points for any animals that might escape. To the left of the gate, running parallel to a thick wall of vegetation that framed the entire perimeter of the farm, were several enclosures housing an array of grazing animals. William thought these animals were utterly captivating and some of the most beautiful on the farm.

William walked alongside each of the enclosures and said “hello” to all of the animals. Firstly, he walked passed the three zebra, which were munching happily on the grass in their enclosure. Next, he greeted the five impala, then the three puku, the three gemsboks, the three eland, the six oribi, the six bushbucks, the seven roan antelope and, finally, the five gazelle. Each different species lived in the same sized compound, where they were fenced in by four and a half metre-high steel fencing. Nowadays, William’s father rarely came over to this side of the farm, relying on William to clean the enclosures out and to provide the animals with fresh water.

Now at the most south-westerly point of the farm, William came across a pair of eight year old twin giraffes which he had named “The Twins” a few years earlier. Their enclosure had only a few patches of grass left on the ground as a result of the giraffes’ constant pacing backwards and forwards. Any emerging shoots of grass were quickly worn away by the pair’s heavy hooves. At the back of their enclosure, there was a high platform on which William would place hay, acacia leaves and carrots for the giraffes to eat.

William was always mesmerised by the giraffes! He would often try to draw their patchwork patterning at the kitchen table with little success, and always struggled to comprehend how such thin and knobbly legs were able to carry the weight of such an impressive neck! The Twins had been born at the farm but their father had sadly passed away seven years ago, and their mother a year after that. In spite of these losses, The Twins had flourished at the farm and were both an impressive sight.

As William gazed at the pair, he wondered whether he should ask his father to find a female to accompany the two males, but he had recently noticed that his father's patience with his requests was wearing thin. William quickly decided that it was safer not to bother and shouted "goodbye" to the pair before moving on from their enclosure.

After checking on the giraffes, William came to a large paddock which ran alongside the majority of the western edge of the farm. Two metre high, solid metal fencing surrounded the enclosure, which was reinforced by rectangular sheets of solid steel. While such an impressive structure prevented William from seeing directly into the enclosure, there was a good reason for such secure holdings. Here lived one of the farm's most dangerous creatures. William walked up a series of steps to a small viewing area which enabled him to safely look into the creature's enclosure. Each step William walked up was greeted with an aggressive snort from within the fencing. As William reached the viewing area, he looked down to see an ill-tempered black rhino already glaring up in his direction. Aggressively, the female rhino appeared to aim her impressively long horn right at William. With her eyes fuelled with fire and her thick skin acting as a shield, she charged forward! The earth trembled as her every stride pounded the ground. Stones and dust flew into the air, until she came to a halt just before the perimeter of her enclosure, right beneath where William was standing. Through the rising cloud of dust, she grunted loudly and trudged off with her back turned to William in a final act of disrespect. This rhino, which had only recently arrived at the farm and was yet to be named, had a good reason to be in a foul mood. She was twelve months pregnant and, with her due date soon approaching, she was clearly unimpressed by her new accommodation and by William's visit.

Making his way across the courtyard and over to the eastern side of the farm, William laughed with joy at the deep, rumbling groans of thirty magnificent tawny lions, securely contained in a total of twelve main enclosures. These enclosures were divided into two rows of six, separated from one another by a single path, around six feet wide, which had been gradually worn down over time. Every one of these twelve enclosures was the same size; a six metre-squared living space equipped with one water trough and two doors. The ground in each enclosure was covered entirely by grass which had been allowed to grow slightly in order to make the lions more comfortable. A short distance away from the main cluster of lion enclosures, in the most south-easterly part of the farm, two smaller enclosures had been created for any ill, injured or pregnant lions at the farm. These acted as a sanctuary for the weaker lions away from the stresses of living in the more crowded main enclosures.

Leisurely, William walked passed each of the main lion enclosures and smiled to himself. Like on most mornings at Anga Farm, the majority of lions were resting peacefully after an excitable night of stalking one another, play-fighting and socialising. In one enclosure, William watched a particularly impressive looking male lion that appeared to be dreaming in the shadows; his thick, regal mane dancing back and forth in the occasional breeze. In the next enclosure, two majestic looking lionesses, which had recently risen from a well-earned rest, patiently watched as a pair of mischievous cubs practiced their hunting technique on their mothers' tails!

Eventually, William came across his father, who was cleaning out the last of the front row of enclosures whilst an inquisitive, adolescent male lion made repeated attempts to steal the shovel! It was not long before the young lion lost interest in the shovel; soon realising it was a worthless cause. The mischievous male then turned his attention to the more interesting looking spade which was standing up in the corner of the enclosure. Much to William's father's annoyance, the male lion made a sudden dash across the enclosure and grabbed the spade in his jaws! Every time William's father approached to try and retrieve the spade, the young male lion would evade capture at the very last moment and dart off to the opposite end of his living area, obviously proud of himself at being able to escape from the clutches of a fully grown human. The lions never failed to captivate William. Even when they appeared dead to the world, they possessed a magic which William believed no other animal on the farm could match. In his eyes, the lions were the undisputed Kings of Africa.

It was not uncommon for William to see his father working in an enclosure unprotected alongside the lions. Every new-born cub at Anga Farm was hand-raised by William's father, enabling him to gain the trust and obedience of the lion from the earliest age possible. On such occasions, William would watch nervously as the fearsome looking lions, which in the wild would not hesitate for a moment to kill any rival who dared to enter his or her territory, did not seem at all bothered by the presence of William's father. At such a young age, William was never allowed to enter any of the lions' enclosures, but he looked forward to the day when he would be old enough to help care for the big cats.

As William walked past the very last lion enclosure towards the northern end of the farm, a small trio of animals fell into a frantic fit of hysteria; their hooting cries only silenced by the threatening growl from a nearby lioness. The three spotted hyenas swirled in a frenzy around their enclosure, collectively rejoicing at the arrival of William. William's father had told his son that the hyenas used to be part of a strong knit clan which totalled four hyenas. The four hyenas had originally belonged to a notorious gang of thieves and debt collectors in the north, who would use them as a means of intimidation and control. Over a period of four years, the hyenas were exposed to a world of violence and crime and the gang would even force the scrawny looking hyenas to perform tricks in the street for some extra money. However, the thugs in the gang were eventually arrested and the local authorities brought the hyena clan to Anga Farm.

Tragically, on their arrival at the farm, one of the hyenas died from complications involving the anaesthetic that was used to sedate the animals during their relocation. Despite this, the surviving three hyenas thrived and over time they managed to form a strong bond. William had been told by his father to keep a distance from these animals as he did not believe that they could ever fully trust people again due to the cruelty they had been subject to before they came to Anga Farm.

Now passed the hyenas' enclosure and at the very northern tip of the farm, William arrived at an old, dilapidated building which housed both the animal food preparation room and a cluttered store room where tools, spare fencing, medicines and cleaning equipment could be found. What William's father did not know was that William was aware that his father also kept three guns hidden there, which William had mistakenly come across two years earlier. At the time when he found them, William was too frightened to ask his father why he needed guns but, as he got older, he realised that they were simply a necessary safety precaution, just in case one of the animals escaped from their enclosure.

Behind the crumbling building, William came to a single enclosure, about the size of a basketball court, which was currently empty. As a young boy, William had noticed it, but did not regard the enclosure as any different to the others scattered around the farm, apart from the obvious difference in size. As he grew older and more inquisitive, William began questioning his father more about the enclosure. One particular meal time around three years ago, William decided to ask his father what the large, empty enclosure was used for. Looking concerned, his father leaned in closer to his son.

"Listen here boy, you're absolutely sure you want to know?" he asked.

"Yes!" William replied enthusiastically, suddenly sitting upright in his chair. Reluctantly, his father explained.

"Right then Will, most people round here would call it a kraal, but we call it the paddock here." Leaning in further, he cautiously continued. "It's an enclosure where the animals are held the day before they are due to leave the farm forever."

"Why do they want to leave? Where do they go?" William whispered, as his eyes began filling up at the thought.

Taking a big gulp of his beer, William's father paused for a moment, staring intently at the kitchen table top, and then continued carefully.
"Well Will…sometimes a zoo, nature reserve or other farm will want to buy one or more of our animals and release them back into the wild or maybe allow more people to see them. I don't know their exact reasons every time. You see boy; this is how we make money. We raise them ourselves from the day they are born, or sometimes we even buy them from neighbouring farms or game reserves in the area. People from zoos, reserves and farms come from all over the world and pay us good money for our animals. The money we're paid by these people puts the food on our table, pays for us to run the farm and keep the other animals."

Seeing tears begin to fall from his son's eyes, William's father grabbed his son's hand.
"I know it's hard but, without selling our animals, we couldn't survive. So you must promise me boy - don't ever get too attached to any of our animals! If you do, saying goodbye will be so much harder." William's father was now staring hard into his son's eyes, watching the tears roll slowly down his cheeks.
"Ok…I'll try," was all William could muster.

As William's father continued to look over the kitchen table at his son, he saw William's eyes full of sadness. It was at that moment that William's father began to understand that he was asking too much of his son. Most young boys his age would naturally become attached to any animal in their care, never mind the beautiful ones that lived on the farm. As a female zebra's cry suddenly rang out in the background, breaking the eerie silence that had filled the kitchen, William's father looked down and realised that his son would never be able to cope with losing those closest to him. The death of his mother had probably affected him more than his father had initially thought, or perhaps he had just never taken the time to notice? Staring at his empty beer bottle, he knew his son would try for him, without question. But William's father knew he had to do something to make this easier on his son.

"Alright then. I'll tell you what I'll do for you!" Sitting up in his chair, William's father looked his son straight in the eye. "Instead of having you around, blubbering all over the farm and causing a scene, on the day someone comes to buy an animal and take them from the paddock, you're going to George's house."

George Etana worked for William's father on the farm and lived locally in the very heart of Anga. William's father always said that George was the only man he would ever trust enough to help him run the farm.
"You'll spend the entire day there. In fact, you can go there the day before the animals leave and come back the next day once they're gone. That's an entire night away from the farm! How good does that sound?" William's father tried to put on his most enthusiastic voice to convince his son that this was a good idea.

While the thought of losing any one of the animals that he loved still clouded William's mind, the possibility of seeing the outside world did seem quite exciting. Eventually, William let out a slight smile and chuckled gently.

"That might be good," he whispered slowly to his father.

"Excellent! I will tell George in the morning!" Relieved, William's father smiled to himself. He had finally found a solution to a problem he had been worrying about since the day William had been born.

CHAPTER THREE

After leaving the paddock at the very northern tip of the farm, William walked back around the ram-shackled food preparation building and, kneeling awkwardly just in front of the food preparation room door, William began to tie one of his unfastened shoelaces. Behind him, he suddenly heard the sound of a slow, carefully placed foot being pressed down on the ground. William continued to kneel down, now pretending to tie his other shoelace. He listened intently. The almost silent sound of stalking feet was still moving deliberately towards him. William continued to play with his lace, pretending to be unaware of the approaching footsteps.

Suddenly, the stalker flung itself forward. William rolled sideways out of harm's way, whilst the stalker fell heavily, face first to the ground. Dusting himself down, William chuckled. "Are you ever going to learn? I could have heard you a mile away, with the racket that you were making!" Lying on the floor, Saba's frustration boiled over and she slammed her hands against the ground.
"I thought I had you! I was this close," she grumbled.

"You weren't close at all! In fact you may be getting worse," William pointed out light-heartedly.
"Whatever!" she snarled back.

Holding his right hand out to help Saba up, William watched in amusement as Saba rather childishly chose to ignore it and instead, clumsily picked herself up and stormed off towards the giraffes' enclosure. *No doubt she'll be plotting another attempt soon*, William thought to himself. As Saba stomped heavily across the courtyard, kicking stones and muttering to herself, William watched and thought back to the first time he ever met Saba Etana.

The pair first met around three years ago when Saba's father, George Etana, brought William back to their house for the first time. A kind and charismatic man, George had worked at the farm for as long as William could remember. On the morning of William's first visit, William had anxiously crossed Anga Farm's central courtyard towards the gate, where George was waiting patiently for him. As the scorching sun warmed the back of William's neck, butterflies swirled around inside of his stomach. For years, William's father had forbidden his son from leaving the farm, claiming that the outside world was "far too dangerous" for a young boy like William. The only glimpse of life outside the farm that William ever caught was when he waited for his father to return to the farm after "seeing a man about a dog." The distant sounds of cars, trucks and motorbikes hurtling along the main track towards Anga's town centre had always terrified William and, as a result, William had never even found the courage to venture more than a few metres down the farm track.

As William continued to make his way towards George, he suddenly caught sight of a moving object in the corner of his eye. Looking to his right, William could just make out an agitated male lion pacing back and forth along the inside fence of the paddock. Even at a distance, William could see his overgrown, shadowy mane swaying in all directions. The day before, William's father had told his son that the male lion was destined for a nature reserve in Johannesburg.
"He has been cooped up surrounded by all those nagging lionesses for too long. He needs some peace and quiet," William's father had explained.

Taking one final look at the male lion, William reassured himself that, whilst the lion was apprehensively pacing back and forth, he had no actual reason to be concerned about what lay in store for him. Soon the male lion would be bounding freely through thick African bush, perhaps defending a territory of his own choosing and maybe even protecting an entire pride of his own. William looked away and continued to walk towards the gate where George was still patiently waiting for him.

William and George strode purposefully through the farm gate, down the long track which led the pair away from the farm until they finally reached the main track which ran towards Anga's town centre. George's longer legs meant that William struggled to keep up at first, but William was determined to remain close to George. The journey to the Etana household was William's first time outside the farm, and he felt understandably wary. Nevertheless, as the pair continued further and further along the side of the main track, William's nerves gradually began to fade away.

Passing by the occasional cluster of stalls, William was mesmerised by the variety of mouth-watering fruits, vibrant clothes and the unusual carvings and sculptures that were on display. The stalls became closer and closer together the further down the track they went and it was not long before George and William were in the very heart of Anga. William nervously looked around as crowds of people pushed by him. Cars blasted their horns furiously at the hordes of prospective buyers, who leisurely strolled across the uneven track without any warning whenever a particular stall caught their eye. William even found himself giggling at the over-enthusiastic Anga market traders, who battled with one another to have the loudest and most extravagant sales pitch.

An hour since they had left the farm, George and William left the bustling epicentre of Anga and walked down a side street which led off the main track. At the end of this street, George stopped and carefully opened a brightly painted purple gate. This was the Etana household.

Initially, the house had been made out of brick, but it had been covered years later with a clay cladding to help protect it from the elements. The front step consisted of two heavy slabs of rock, placed on top of each other, and the wooden door had started to wear away in the top right-hand corner, allowing air to pass freely in and out of the house. There was a row of three small windows at the front of the house, each framed by hand embroidered white cotton curtains.

Walking towards the front door, William suddenly felt the butterflies beginning to swarm inside his stomach again as he grew increasingly uneasy at the thought of meeting the entire

Etana family. As George pulled open the flimsy door, he turned back to William and smiled. Bending down to William's level, he whispered reassuringly.
"When you're in my house, I want you to feel like you are in your own home. We will treat you as one of the family, as long as that's ok with you?" Seemingly sensing William's nerves, George decided to give William a helping hand, and he placed a supportive arm around him, gently guiding him through the front door and into the main room.

Immediately, William was faced with Saba's mother, Zaria Etana, who had hurried across the room when she had heard the squeaking of their gate. An enormous lady, Zaria was dressed from head to toe in a multi-coloured garb, and now towered over William.
"Oh my goodness! You must be the heir to the throne, the one and only Prince William!" Laughing hysterically to herself, Zaria began shaking William's hand enthusiastically. "Good grief, it is a pleasure to finally meet you your highness. I have heard a lot about you from one of your most humble subjects." Still laughing manically to herself, Zaria nodded in the direction of an amused George, as a stunned William remained speechless. "Well, a future King must meet a future Queen!" Holding a confused William by the hand, Zaria escorted him over to one of the two sofas in the main room. Sitting alone, shyly looking in the opposite direction, sat Saba Etana. "Now I'm going to make you a feast fit for a future King! George, I need a servant!" Grabbing George by the hand, Zaria dragged her husband off towards the kitchen, still howling with laughter, leaving William and Saba sitting alone together.

Still looking away, William noticed Saba's fingers gripping the end of her chair tightly. Detecting her nerves, William tried to break the ice.
"I think your mum's a little confused, she thinks I'm a Prince. Worst still, she thinks I'm a future King!"
"Oh she's crazy! You'll get used to her though," Saba replied casually.
"I'm William, nice to meet you!" Holding his hand out, William smiled broadly hoping to make a good impression.
"I know that, stupid! I think the entire street will know your name after your royal reception from my mother," Saba responded, ignoring William's handshake.
"Oh yeah! Well…it's nice to meet you anyway." William felt this was not going well when Saba raised her eyebrows at his extreme politeness.
"So, what do you like doing?" William persisted.
"Nothing!" Saba replied defiantly.
"You must like something!"
"Absolutely nothing!" Saba confirmed.
"Ok then." William conceded defeat and turned away, deciding to study the family pictures on the wall. Noticing his disappointment, Saba suddenly felt enormously guilty. After a few seconds of awkward silence, Saba eventually gave in.
"Well, I like animals. That's about it!"
"Really?" William exclaimed excitedly. "I love animals! My father owns the farm that your father works at and I get to work with animals all day long! What animals do you like?" William could not hide his enthusiasm. Finally he had met someone his own age, and she liked animals just like him!
"I absolutely love giraffes! They're my favourite!" Saba cried out.
"Wow, we have two at the farm! The Twins! Their mother

and father sadly died soon after they were born, but they're incredible. You must come and see them sometime!"

Overhearing the conversation, George had wandered back into the room.
"Dad, you never told me you worked with giraffes! You said that all you did everyday was shepherd goats!" Saba fired an accusing look in George's direction. For a moment, George seemed completely lost for words at William's revelation. However, George quickly promised Saba that if it was alright with William's father, she could soon come up to the farm and visit them, hoping to distract Saba away from his obvious deception.
"Sure it will be fine!" William declared, imagining what it would be like to finally have company his own age at the farm.

For the rest of that evening and throughout the next day, William and Saba swapped tales about their love for animals, their families and about their childhoods so far. William remained speechless as Saba told elaborate tales about her visits to the market, trekking through the bush with her father and the daily routine of being schooled at home by her mother.

The day after William had first arrived, Zaria cooked a delicious beef bobotie for dinner. William and Saba cleaned the dishes afterwards, then George announced it was time he took William back to the farm. When saying their goodbyes, Saba eagerly reminded both William and George that they had promised she could soon go to the farm to meet the giraffes.

"A promise is a promise!" she warned. Zaria wrapped her arms lovingly around William until he could not breathe any longer, and said she looked forward to the day he would return. Whilst William watched George say goodbye to Zaria and Saba, promising them both that he would not be too long and embracing the pair at the same time, William could not help feeling jealous. He really wished his mother was still alive, and that she would care for him as Zaria obviously did for her family.

In that lonely moment, William pondered what his mother might have been like. *Would she have been as loving and as welcoming as Zaria? Would they all, as a family, have cleaned the dishes after eating a meal together? Would she miss him when he helped his father around the farm?* The squeaking of the gate which George had pushed open suddenly broke William's train of thought. Suddenly aware of his surroundings, William turned to wave goodbye to Zaria and Saba, and he hoped that this would not be the last time he would be visiting their house.

Throughout the three years that followed their initial meeting, Saba and William visited one another regularly. Eventually, George was forced to bring Saba to the farm everyday (much to the delight of William) after Zaria had got a job as a receptionist at the local health clinic and could no longer look after her daughter full-time. As time went by, both William and Saba had the privilege of getting to know all of the extraordinary animals at Anga Farm. They were also there for one another for the occasional heartbreak of having to say goodbye to animals they had come to regard as good friends.

Now, as William approached the giraffes' enclosure after

surviving Saba's earlier ambush attempt, he found her leaning against the metal fencing, watching closely as the giraffes elegantly wandered over towards their feeding platform. Saba was the only other person William had ever met who could be entirely spellbound by the beauty of an animal, marvelling at their every move, however insignificant it might be to others. For that reason alone, as William joined Saba watching the giraffes devouring their lunchtime snack, he knew he had a friend for life.

CHAPTER FOUR

"Hey! Boy!" William's father barked from across the courtyard, his bulky frame clearly visible alongside the lion enclosures. "George and I need your help over here."
"It sounds like I've got work to do, Saba." As William crossed the courtyard, leaving Saba behind to start cleaning out the zebras' enclosure, William noticed his father holding a brown, leather collar and a robust looking metal chain dangling down towards the ground.
"Are we moving Bahiya?" William asked as he now stood opposite George and his father.
"The vet came two days ago and said she's around three and a half months gone now. Your father thinks it's time we should move her so she can get some peace and quiet," George smiled back. "You get the door, I'll take the fire extinguisher." William nodded in acknowledgement as he made his way over to the nearest of the two doors that every enclosure at the farm had in order to gain access.

Lying dozily across the ground, a seven year old lioness sunbathed in the scorching rays of the mid-morning sun, her tail flicking from side to side among the shoots of grass. The sound of the lioness's heavy, laboured breathing was joined by the aggravated groans of an adult male in the neighbouring pen, who used to be the lioness's loyal companion until they were separated just before the vet's recent visit. The agitated male patrolled the interior fence that separated his living area from that of the snoozing lioness. His thick, unkempt mane rubbed against the metal fencing and his wild eyes stared furiously as William's father dared to edge closer and closer to the enclosure containing his former companion.

The jealous male suddenly released his aggression on an unsuspecting adolescent who shared his enclosure, striking out with his enormous paw at the much smaller male who had foolishly approached to see what was irritating the larger male. The noise that had erupted from this conflict caused the pregnant lioness to move to the furthest corner of her enclosure and away from the commotion.

Since the day she was born, the lioness had spent every moment on the farm in an enclosed area. Her mother had immediately refused to feed both her and her two brothers at birth, so William's father had intervened earlier than normal and started hand-raising the cubs himself. Whilst the female had managed to survive, it was too late for her two little brothers, who were too weak. They both died two days after their birth. Since then, the female had grown into a stunning lioness, whose laid-back temperament was a testament to the close bond she had developed with William's father. As a result of this, she was the only animal on the farm that William's father had himself given an actual name. Her Swahili name – Bahiya – meant *the beautiful one.*

After William carefully unlocked the door into Bahiya's enclosure, he opened it only partially so as not to startle the sleeping lioness. His father then entered, promptly followed by George who vigilantly kept watch, the fire extinguisher in hand and aimed in the direction of the lioness in case of an emergency. Fire extinguishers were primarily used as a safety precaution, always on hand when William's father entered an animal's enclosure. A single blast from the extinguisher would startle an animal, allowing William's father and George the opportunity to safely exit the enclosure. William only hoped that George would not have to use it today.

Whilst William's father had developed a special bond with Bahiya, he still approached her with caution. "A pregnant lioness is the most dangerous kind of lion, Will!" his father always warned. "Never, ever approach her unless you really have to."

Upon hearing footsteps close by, Bahiya rose lethargically from her slumber, her eyes never leaving William's father as she padded sluggishly towards him. Meeting in the centre of her living space, the lioness rubbed her head affectionately against the muscular arm of William's father, which he wrapped lovingly around Bahiya's neck. Bahiya then allowed William's father to carefully wrap the leather collar around her neck, which William's father quickly did. He then securely attached the metal chain to create a lead, made to manage the power of a fully-grown lioness.

Just when William's father was ready to lead Bahiya out of the enclosure, the lioness suddenly rooted herself to the ground, refusing to cooperate. Whilst the two had developed a close bond over the years, Bahiya still liked to occasionally reinforce her dominance. After a short spell of stubbornness, which also required a great deal of patience from William's father, Bahiya finally decided to oblige. Reluctantly, the lioness got to her feet and walked alongside William's father, who directed her towards the door out of the enclosure, which William dutifully opened. George shadowed the pair with the fire extinguisher as they carefully made their way through the door and towards the two smaller enclosures, situated about fifty feet away in the south-east corner of the farm.

In the distance, the door to Bahiya's new residence had already been opened, allowing the lioness a glimpse into her new, spacious accommodation. As she advanced, her steps became more measured, her head became lower to the ground, and she sniffed to try to detect any scents left behind by the previous occupants. She paused in the doorway, her right paw raised slightly off the ground. Slowly, moving her head into the enclosure, she assessed her new living area, checking every corner for any potential threats. Once satisfied, Bahiya carefully took her first steps into the enclosure.

"Ok bro," William's father whispered to George. George then quietly placed the fire extinguisher on the ground and gently closed the enclosure door, shutting in both the lioness and William's father. As William looked on, his father patiently led Bahiya around her new living quarters, giving her the time to adjust to the new sights, smells and sounds. In the far right corner of the enclosure stood a one metre tall wooden birthing den, which had been filled with fresh straw in order to allow the lioness somewhere comfortable to lie during labour.

It was not long before Bahiya became accustomed to her surroundings, and William's father detached the metal chain lead and removed her collar.
"Good girl," he whispered softy whilst stroking the lioness's neck.

George could not help but laugh to himself at how much Bahiya was enjoying the attention from William's father.
"I think she'll be fine in here," said William's father, as he patted Bahiya softly on the side of her stomach. "See you later girl."

Once William's father had exited the enclosure, he muttered, "Thanks boy," in the direction of his son and then set off across the courtyard towards the farmhouse, telling George he was "seeing a man about a dog for a minute." George and William remained silent for several minutes, both captivated by the sight of Bahiya wandering around her new enclosure, attempting to familiarise herself with her new surroundings. Eventually, it was George who broke the silence.
"She's beautiful, no?"
"Of course!" William agreed. "How long do you think it will be before she gives birth?"
"Who knows these things?" George declared as he nodded towards the sky. "I think she will be in there for at least another week yet."
"Really?" William replied, unable to hide his obvious disappointment.
"Be patient boy," George laughed, placing his arm around

William. "But you know something: your father was saying he thinks it will be sooner. He thinks it will be tonight!" George scoffed at the suggestion. "But, as you know, he's always been a bit crazy!" Laughing out loud, George turned away from William, patted him on the back and made his way over to the farmhouse, claiming, "I'm going to see how your father is doing with that dog."

Alone, outside Bahiya's new enclosure, William took a step closer. Carefully, he studied Bahiya. Lying in the birthing den, the lioness squirmed restlessly, searching for the perfect spot to settle down for the afternoon. Every time William saw Bahiya, she always reminded him why his father had named her, *the beautiful one.* Shimmering, her deep, piercing eyes stared around her enclosure as she continued to fidget amongst the straw. Captured by her spell, William found himself drifting deeper into Bahiya's eyes. He thought back to the conversation he had with his father about three years ago at the kitchen table. William could still hear his father's words as clear as the night he first spoke them.
"Don't get too attached to these animals, Will!"

William wondered to himself whether his father would ever actually sell Bahiya for money. *Was the love he showed for her real or just an act? Was it just an act which he put together to get Bahiya to obey him?* As William sat down in front of the lioness's new enclosure, he could not understand, if his father had become so attached to Bahiya, how he could ever expect William not to do the same?

"I just don't get it!" William muttered to himself in frustration, failing to understand how on earth his father could ever sell one of the animals he had worked so hard to raise to adulthood. William grabbed a large clump of grass from beneath him and tore it away from the ground. Just as William had started to question his father's motives, he heard a familiar voice behind him.

"How is she doing?" Saba asked as she approached William.

"Oh she's fine, just trying to get comfy. How did the cleaning go?" William replied, as he threw the clump of grass into the air.

"That's why I'm here. I cleaned the zebras' water trough and re-filled it, but I can't find the shovel for the muck."

Shaking his head and laughing loudly, William responded. "You can never find it, even though I keep telling you it is kept in the first cupboard on your left in the store room. I don't know why you don't just admit that you're too sensitive to the smell of zebra muck!"

"I am not too sensitive to the smell of zebra muck!" Saba roared back in defiance, hitting William in the arm as hard as she could.

"All right, calm down. I'll do it!" William exclaimed as he started to make his way back to the store room, with Saba following, smirking to herself.

For the remainder of the afternoon, Saba and William spent their time cleaning out the grazers' enclosures, often taking breaks to check up on how Bahiya was doing. Every time they approached the lioness's enclosure, they both secretly hoped to hear the yelping of a newly born cub. However, on every occasion they would leave disappointed. The most active they ever found Bahiya was when she was squirming uncontrollably in her sleep!

Once Saba and William had finished cleaning out the grazers' enclosures, the pair made their way over to the food-preparation room to see if they could help George and William's father with the late-afternoon feeds. As far as Saba and William were concerned, this was the most exciting job on the farm as it involved throwing large pieces of meat into the lion and hyena enclosures. Saba and William loved to see the reactions of the animals as the meat landed in their enclosures. Every time, chaos would break out as the animals would compete mercilessly with one another for the best pieces of meat. High-pitched squeals and deep, rumbling growls would erupt as every animal fought for their share of the spoils. Saba and William found the whole performance rather entertaining!

As they entered the food-preparation room, they noticed George packing the wheelbarrow with the meat he had just prepared. Strangely though, there was no sign of William's father.

"Where's my father?" William asked George.

"Gone out for a while and don't ask me where because I don't know. I bet it has something to do with a dog though!" George chuckled to himself. William had become accustomed to his father's unannounced excursions from the farm of late, so he decided that there was no point asking George any more questions.

As well as being an extremely raucous event, feeding the thirty lions and the three hyenas was also very strenuous. With only a single wheelbarrow, five or more trips were often needed to feed all of the animals, so a strategy was required to make it easier. On this occasion, Saba took over packing the meat into the wheelbarrow and William then steered it to where George was patiently waiting to throw it into the clutches of a waiting animal.

Once, William had asked George why both he and William's father never entered the enclosures during feeding time. George had bluntly replied.
"William, normally these animals are my friends. They tolerate me going into their space because they know I won't do them any harm. But when food is suddenly thrown in, they would no longer see me as a friend, but as a thief threatening to steal their food! They would think nothing of attacking me to protect their meal." Noticing William's concerned face, George had tried to reassure him. "They're just following their instincts William! It's safer for us to stay on this side of the fence."

When all of the lions and hyenas had been catered for and the roars and cackles had subsided, George and Saba decided that it was time to head home. William's father was still nowhere to be seen, so William decided to check up on Bahiya one final time. As the evening sun started to fade, William made his way over to the two smaller enclosures to find the lioness sleeping soundly in her birthing den, surrounded by straw. On closer inspection, William noticed that, while Bahiya had helped herself to a large amount of water from the trough in her enclosure, the lioness had not touched the meat which George had thrown into her enclosure earlier on. Concerned, William made a mental note to tell his father about this the moment he arrived back at the farm. Realising that it was getting late, William made his way back to the farmhouse kitchen to get something to eat.

The farm's kitchen was typical of most others in the area. It was small in size, with cupboard doors made from locally salvaged wood. Most of the handles had fallen off these cupboards over the years. The tiles that decorated the walls were a faded yellow colour, and a flickering light bulb hung from the ceiling, partially illuminating a rectangular wooden table in the centre of the room. On the table, William saw an old knife, a wooden chopping block and two empty plastic bowls which looked as if their last wash had not been as thorough as it should have been. The two bowls also reminded William of the large mound of dirty plates stacked behind him in the sink. William picked up one of the plastic bowls and walked passed the kitchen table towards the rusty, food stained hob. He lifted the lid off a large metal pan and used his bowl to scoop out a small portion of the left-over beef stew that his father had made two days ago. With both William and his father often working long hours on the farm, it was more practical to cook a large pan of food like a stew, which they could just serve themselves whenever they had the time to eat. William took his stew, wiped the side of the bowl with his fingers, then went to sit in his father's favourite chair in the farm's moderately sized sitting room.

William quickly ate his stew and made himself comfortable. He began to wonder how many cubs Bahiya would have. Earlier that day, William's father had told him that this was Bahiya's first litter so they would usually only be expecting a single cub. However, he said that, on occasions, first time mothers could give birth to more. William wondered what the future would hold for Bahiya's litter. *Would they eventually be sold to a zoo, farm or nature reserve? Would his father decide not to sell Bahiya's litter because of the close bond between the pair?* It was late and William suddenly felt overcome with exhaustion. William shifted his weight in the chair to find a more comfortable sitting position. He closed his eyes, happy to finally get some rest after a long day working at the farm.

Suddenly, out of the darkness, the silhouette of a pale lion appeared in front of William. The lion, which William guessed to be quite young due to its short mane, stared furiously in William's direction. Sub-consciously realising he must be dreaming, William did not feel scared. He was curious as to why the lion was so upset. The lion approached closer and closer to within only a few metres of William. Finally, William was close enough to see into the lion's eyes: they burned with rage! William could not understand why the pale lion was so angry with him. The lion let out a low growl, partially opening its mouth to reveal its razor sharp teeth. William was now frozen to the spot. He began to panic, desperate to wake up. William wanted to run away, to escape. The lion's growl exploded into a thundering roar! Lowering its shoulders, the pale beast revealed its terrifying fangs and launched itself into the air towards William. Just before the lion collided with William, it opened its mouth wide and roared magnificently. The lion's thundering breath forced William backwards. He closed his eyes shut, ready for the pain. But it did not come. Instead, there was only silence.

William woke to find himself clinging tightly to the chair's arm-rests. Sweat dripped down the sides of his forehead. His heart pounded loudly in his chest.
"It was only a dream. It was only a dream," William reassured himself, trying to catch his breath. Chuckling to himself, William could not believe how realistic the dream had felt.

For a moment, he actually felt as if the lion was going to kill him.

Suddenly, William remembered the mound of dirty plates stacked precariously in the kitchen sink and the promise he had made his father to clean them. However, no matter how hard William tried to lift himself from the chair, his body refused to allow it. Exhaustion had taken over and, before he knew it, his eyes were closed and he had once again fallen asleep in his father's chair.

CHAPTER FIVE

"Hey Will, wake up!" William's father yelled as he shook his son repeatedly.

"What?" Half awake, William replied only faintly. Rubbing his eyes, he had yet to figure out whether this was another of his unusual dreams.

"It's a miracle. A miracle has happened!" His father announced.

"What? Who's a miracle?" Yawning, William stretched both his arms and legs out, enjoying the feeling for a moment before eventually replying. The urgency of his father seemed lost on William. "What do you mean a miracle?"

"It's indescribable! You have to come and see it for yourself."

Sluggishly getting to his feet, William followed his father out of the sitting room and into the kitchen. The normally dim light seemed brighter than usual, blinding William for just a moment, until his eyes adjusted. Immediately, William saw that his father was dressed in his work overalls. He was rummaging furiously through a kitchen drawer next to the sink, looking for something. Looking out of the kitchen window, William noticed that it was pitch black outside. *It must be really late,* William thought to himself.

"What time is it?" William mumbled, combining it with another yawn.

"I think it's around 5am," his father replied. "Got it! Finally!" As William's father turned around with a second torch in his hand, William was startled to see two large blood-stained patches, one on each of his father's thighs.

"What's happened?" William panicked. "Are you hurt?"

"No Will," his father reassured. "It's Bahiya. She's given birth to a cub, a little boy I think! It's not…it's not your usual lion cub though!" William's father struggled to hide his enthusiasm. "Just come with me and you will see." Grabbing his son by the hand, William's father passed him the spare torch and guided him out of the back door and into the night.

As soon as they were outside, William detected an entirely different atmosphere around the farm to the one he had experienced earlier that day. In the dark, William could see nothing. He could just hear the unnerving sounds of animals all around him. Hyenas shrieked loudly behind him. Lions growled at one another in front of him. To his left, he heard the gate rattling in its hinges. The rhino snorted louder than William had ever heard before. Hyenas began to laugh manically.

Despite his father guiding him, William had no idea where he was. The young boy tried desperately to use his torch to help him gather his bearings, but the light was very dim. William suddenly stopped and let go of his father's hand. To his left, a whole group of shimmering lights bounced back in his direction. Immediately, William knew this must be the lions.

Their fearsome eyes moved back and forth, up and down, all glaring in William's direction. They appeared almost like an excitable swarm of fireflies dancing in the night sky. Even though William could only see the lions' eyes, he had never seen them this active before. Out of the darkness, William suddenly felt something grab his right arm.
"Come on Will," his father whispered. The pair moved on quickly. As they passed the two rows of lion enclosures, William finally caught the faintest glimpse of the lions. Inside their enclosures, the lions were pacing back and forth, keeping their eyes fixed on both William and his father.
"They're in hunting mode!" whispered William's father.
"What do you mean?" William replied.
"At night they become more active and any sounds, like the ones we're making, instantly triggers their hunting instincts." William's father spoke softly, yet his voice appeared to ring out around the farm. "But just ignore them. In the morning they'll be back to their lazy selves again." William's father chuckled to himself, leaving his son in a state of shock. It had been a long time since William had heard his father laugh!

Eventually, the pair came to the area where Bahiya's enclosure was. Despite the raucous atmosphere, this area still felt calm and secluded and William could now see why his father had placed the two smaller enclosures here. As they neared the enclosure housing Bahiya, William's father signalled for his son to be quiet, so as not to disturb her. William could not contain his excitement. His hands were trembling! Even though he was tiptoeing, his feet sounded louder than ever. With only a few feet to go, William's father suddenly placed his hand on his son's shoulder and stopped him from moving any closer to Bahiya. Gently, William's father knelt down and looked into his son's eyes.

"Now listen here boy. What you are about to see, you have to promise me that you will never tell anyone about it! Do you understand me?" The sudden change in his father's tone shocked William and he immediately stood up straight.
"Of course" William replied, wondering what on earth was going on.
"You promise Will!" The force of his father's breath against William's face let William know that his father was being deadly serious.
"I promise," William whispered back.
"Right then." William's father led his son closer to the edge of Bahiya's enclosure.

Before William could even see the lioness, he could hear her slow, heavy breathing in the dark. William peered through the steel fencing, searching for the lioness. Eventually, he could just make out her outline. In the birthing den, Bahiya was lying down, her front legs laid out in front of her and her back facing William and his father. On hearing their arrival, Bahiya looked back over her shoulder to inspect the visitors. In the darkness, Bahiya's eyes shimmered. However, instead of appearing fearsome, William thought they were shining with pride. Seemingly realising that it was William and his father, Bahiya quickly settled back down to rest, assured that the visitors meant her no harm.

Out of the darkness, a flash of light appeared from behind Bahiya's stomach. However, as soon as it had arrived, it had gone. Immediately, William glanced at his father.
"Keep looking," he whispered and he nodded in the direction

of Bahiya. William quickly looked again, straining his eyes through the darkness. Once more, a white light shot up from behind Bahiya's stomach, then disappeared again.

Confused, William continued to examine the enclosure, hoping to find the cub and hoping to see the mysterious light one more time. The relative calm within the enclosure was suddenly disturbed as Bahiya lifted her head and began to get to her feet.
"Wow!" William gasped.

CHAPTER SIX

Squirming underneath Bahiya, illuminating the entire birthing den, was a pure white lion cub. The little cub cried out, obviously searching for its mother who had started to make her way over to the water trough in the opposite corner of her enclosure. The cub's white fur shone in the night sky like a blazing star. Bahiya looked back at her cub, watching it attentively. As it was a new-born, the cub manoeuvred itself clumsily, struggling to locate where its mother was in the dark. At less than thirty centimetres long and weighing only half a kilogram, the cub yelped once again as it wriggled amongst the straw bedding. Realising that her cub was looking for her, Bahiya settled back down into her birthing den in front of her little cub. The ray of light disappeared, leaving William and his father in the dark once again.

"What is it?" William whispered.
"It is a white lion cub! They're very rare! Very rare indeed! I have only ever heard of them being born in an area called Timbavati, many miles south of here," his father replied quietly, trying not to disturb Bahiya.

"But how…what…why has Bahiya given birth to one?"
"I have no idea Will, but I always knew Bahiya was a special lioness!" William's father whispered back.

The pair remained vigilant, not daring to leave the enclosure in case they missed another chance to see the magical new arrival. William's father placed an affectionate arm around his son. William could not remember the last time his father had shown him this type of affection. Whilst Bahiya repositioned herself amongst the straw, William and his father caught another glimpse of the glowing white cub. Its beauty transfixed them.

"You know, Will, I might need your help looking after this cub," William's father whispered out of the darkness. These few words sent William into a sudden fit of excitement.
"Oh please, please, please let me help!" William cried out, causing Bahiya to glance disapprovingly over her shoulder, in William's direction.
"Ok, but you do know a lion cub requires a lot of care. This is no joke. You will need to feed it every four hours to begin with, regardless of whether it is day or night," William's father warned.
"I don't care about sleep! I promise I will never forget to feed it!" William was now becoming increasingly animated, bouncing up and down in front of his father. "Please say you will let me help!"
"Alright then, Will," his father agreed. For the first time in many years, William threw his arms without hesitation around his father, as tears of joy rolled down his cheeks.
"Thank you so much!" William whispered into his father's chest. Time seemed to stand still as the pair remained in their

embrace. Still in his father's arms, William looked up and marvelled at the stars which decorated the night sky. William thought they seemed to be burning brighter than normal, almost as if they too were celebrating the miracle birth that night at Anga Farm.

"What could possibly have happened that you would need to call me out of bed at this time of night?" George's voice immediately interrupted the period of calm that had temporarily settled upon the farm. Even the lions and hyenas had settled down for a short period, getting some rest after the earlier excitement. William and his father turned around. From the darkness, George suddenly appeared.
"You know, my friend, Mrs Etana was not impressed! A beautiful person in the day she might be, but when it is time to sleep she turns into a monster. This better be worth…"

George's rant came to an immediate stop. Bahiya had momentarily left her new-born cub to take another well deserved drink of water from the trough. William watched George as he appeared to be frozen to the spot. His eyes were fixed on the bright white cub which was still squirming amongst the straw in the birthing den. As if he did not trust what he was seeing, George leant in for a closer look. William noticed George's hands shaking slightly as they rested on the steel fencing.
"It can't be!" George murmured under his breath. William had never seen George like this before. His eyes never once left the cub as he spoke.
"I can't explain it, but it is definitely a white lion cub," William's father replied. His father's serious tone immediately caught William's attention. Again, his father's mood had

changed within a matter of seconds. No-one said anything. They all glared into Bahiya's enclosure at the cub, who was yelping for its nearby mother to return. Hearing its distress, Bahiya immediately padded back and settled down in the birthing den, shielding the new arrival from the trio of onlookers. George immediately looked downwards. He focussed intently on the ground beneath him. He appeared lost in his own thoughts. To William, George seemed upset – as if the birth of the white lion cub distressed him deeply.

"It is great news is it not bro?" The silence was broken by William's father.
Gulping heavily, George broke out with his trademark smile. "I am very happy for you both! You have been truly blessed with a miracle." William was confused. Moments earlier, George had appeared heartbroken, as if he had been given some terrible news. But now, George seemed elated.
"You will help me and the boy raise it won't you George?" William's father stared hard at George as he spoke.
"It would be an honour to serve a child of God, my friend." George replied.
"What?" William laughed out loud, once again acquiring Bahiya's disapproval from within the birthing den. "What do you mean, a child of God, George? It's a lion cub!" William continued.
Chuckling to himself, George ruffled William's hair and replied.
"A wise old man once told me, when I was a young boy like you, that white lions are children of a God, sent to earth to help us. They are made out of pure light William. You should never, ever harm a white lion! Ever! The old man told me that if you harm a white lion, you harm the land." George

now turned back to look into Bahiya's enclosure. The lioness remained spread out in her birthing den, now sleeping soundly. "They are a beacon of hope for us all!" George whispered.

For a few moments, the trio remained silent as they all watched Bahiya sleep in her enclosure. George finally broke the quiet.
"So, you see William, it would be an honour for me to help raise this little one."
William was eager to ask more questions about the wise old man and how he knew so much about white lions. However, his father quickly intervened.
"Should we get the little cub out, bro?"
"What do you mean?" William said, confused.
William's father looked down at his son as he replied.
"If we are going to raise it, Will, we need to take it into the house as quickly as possible and feed it." After he spoke, William's father began to walk away from Bahiya's enclosure.
"But won't Bahiya be upset if we take her cub away?" William asked, confused by the need to take the little lion away from Bahiya so soon after it had been born. William's father immediately stopped walking and turned around to face his son. William could see he was angry from the look in his eyes.
"Listen, Will. We decided together that we would take care of the cub, didn't we?" His father's mood had changed once again. The tone of his voice was sharp and to the point. William's question had clearly angered his father.
"I guess so." William replied, in some way understanding the point his father was trying to make.
"You want to work with the lions on the farm in the future, don't you?" William's father approached his son as he spoke

and crouched down to make eye contact with him. The glare in his father's eyes made William's back stiffen up and the hairs on his arms stand on end. A few seconds passed by before William could think clearly enough to respond.
"You know I want to," William muttered. He knew exactly what his father was about to say.
"Well then, this is what we have to do. George and I have been hand-raising every new-born at this farm for years now and this one, however special it may be, will be no different!"

William's father began to walk away again. Whilst William could not help but think that it was cruel to take a new-born cub away from its mother, he also really wanted to work with the lions. This was his opportunity! However cruel it seemed to take the cub away from Bahiya, William could not resist the temptation of helping to hand raise his very own white lion cub!
"Are you coming then?" William's father asked, his outline barely visible in the darkness. William picked himself up and decided that, however hard it would be to watch Bahiya have her cub taken away from her, it would be worth it to help raise the cub himself. William followed his father and George in the darkness as they went to find a piece of meat to lure Bahiya away from her newly born cub.

Twenty minutes later, the trio had returned to Bahiya's enclosure. Quietly, George made his way over to the left hand side of Bahiya's enclosure and pierced a chunk of beef with a long sharp wooden stick. The instrument was often used at the farm, similar to a skewer, to feed the carnivores small pieces of meat. George carefully placed the stick through the steel cage and called the lioness's name repeatedly, hoping to

attract her attention.
"Bahiya, look what I've got! Come on girl!" On hearing his call, Bahiya casually raised her head and inquisitively looked over to where George was standing. Having not eaten for some time, William knew the lioness would find the temptation of a meal hard to resist. Bahiya glanced at her cub, which lay beside her, sleeping soundly in the straw. Eventually, Bahiya lethargically rose to her feet and ambled over to where George was positioned. Immediately, the lioness went for the meat, which she keenly ripped off the stick and eagerly began to devour. With only a short window of opportunity, William carefully opened the enclosure door, whilst his father made his way over to the birthing den where the cub lay asleep.

On hearing his footsteps, Bahiya quickly looked back. However, as it was William's father in her enclosure, who she trusted, the lioness deemed there to be no threat, so she continued to gnaw at her meat. William's father effortlessly scooped up the little cub into his arms and quickly made his way back out of the enclosure. He placed the cub into a giant bucket and gently wrapped it in a soft, brown towel. Both he and his son then made their way hurriedly over to the farmhouse, whilst George went to return the feeding stick to the food-preparation room. William began to hear the frantic whimpers of the newly born cub calling out from inside the bucket. Then, as the pair made their way up the steps and into the farmhouse kitchen, William suddenly heard the unmistakable, distressed calls of Bahiya - the lioness had realised her cub was no longer there!

A few minutes later, George came through the back door and

into the kitchen, where he found William's father shaking a milk bottle over the kitchen sink. William was sat at the kitchen table, his face pale with shock. The lioness's calls of desperation had become more frantic, and they could be heard clearly, even within the farmhouse. George noticed William, who was slumped in his chair, looking up at the window. William's eyes were beginning to well up at the desperate calls coming from outside.
"Tea in the pot?" George asked.
"I think so," William's father replied, checking the scales on his milk bottle without looking up at George.

George made his way over towards the kettle and, as he passed William, he placed a supportive hand on his shoulder. William looked up. Tears were now beginning to spill down his cheeks. George leant down quietly so as not to attract the attention of William's father. He smiled at William and mouthed silently.
"Don't worry. She will be fine tomorrow. I promise you." William looked down at the ground which seemed blurry through the pools in his eyes. William pulled his sleeve over his right hand and used his frayed jumper cuff to wipe the tears from his face.
"I hope so." William whimpered as he looked back up at George.

"Right then!" His father's interruption caused William to sit straight up in his chair. Even George seemed slightly startled. "Let's get you feeding a lion for the first time!" Smiling, William's father seemed completely unaware of the fact that William was upset.
"Really?" William responded cheerfully, wiping his eyes once

more and taking a deep breath. William got up from the chair to follow his father into the sitting room then, suddenly, he froze. Bahiya's agonising groans could be heard once again from outside. William glanced down for just a moment, then raised his head and nodded purposefully, as if to give himself some courage. William made his way through the kitchen and into the sitting room, with George following shortly behind.

William watched in awe as his father carefully scooped the wriggling white cub out of the bucket. Again, William gasped at its beauty. The tiny cub's snow-like fur was even more breath-taking up close.

"Right Will, you have to hold a cub firmly. Wrap one arm around it and use the other to hold the bottle when you feed it." William felt his father's eyes examining him, weighing up one last time whether he had made the right decision to let his son do this. As much as William wanted to look up at his father and tell him that he was ready, William simply could not take his eyes off the white cub.

Gently, William's father lowered the cub into the arms of his son. William was initially staggered by the power of the little cub, as it squirmed in his arms. However, William gripped the wriggling cub tightly with his right arm, and reached out for the bottle which his father was holding nearby.

"You ok, Will?" William's father asked with some concern.

"I'm fine, honest!" William replied. Tentatively, William's father gave the bottle to his son.

After a few failed attempts, the restless cub finally began to suckle on the bottle. William smiled to himself as he felt the cub relax in his arms. Looking up, he noticed his father and George smiling back at him. It was then that he heard Bahiya again. Her calls had now become less frequent, but they still hurt William. Looking down at the cub, he suddenly felt ashamed of himself. William could not believe how selfish he had been! *How can I be so happy when Bahiya must be heartbroken? But then again, is my father right? Was this really for the best?* William looked down at the white cub in his arms, now suckling peacefully on the bottle. To William, the cub seemed content. George also said that Bahiya would soon be alright. William thought that perhaps he should not feel so bad after all. William looked back down at the cub, its eyes not yet open. *It was for the best!* William thought to himself.

"It's empty now Will." William looked up. Standing over him, his father and George were both smiling. William looked back down at the bottle and noticed that it was indeed empty. This did not stop the cub from continuing to suckle on it enthusiastically. In fact, William had to work quite hard to prize the cub away from the bottle!
"What do we do now?" William asked, as he tried to reposition the squirming cub in his arms.
"You William - not us! You will have to make it go to the toilet!" William looked up in horror at his father's suggestion. George and his father suddenly burst out laughing! They laughed so loud it roared through the entire farmhouse. William continued to stare at the pair in a state of shock!

Ten minutes later, William was rubbing the little lion's bottom with some tissues in order to help it go to the toilet! He certainly did not think he would be doing that when he woke up that morning! George explained to William that the young cub needed to be weighed after every feeding session and that William needed to record the cub's weight and toilet activity in a dairy.

"You have to do this every four hours, Will. It is a lot of responsibility. Are you absolutely sure you want to do this?" William's father asked as his son was recording the weight of the cub in an old notebook which George had found in the kitchen.

"I am absolutely sure!" William answered enthusiastically as he finished writing the first diary entry. Behind him, George carefully placed the white lion cub back into the bucket and onto the soft, brown towel where it squirmed to find the perfect resting position.

"What are we going to call it?" William suddenly asked in a rush of excitement. "We've not even thought of a name yet!"

"**It!**" George replied. "The **it** is actually a **him**, William. What are we going to call **him**?"

"Well," William's father chuckled to himself, before continuing. "It's your cub, what do you want to call him?"

William was lost for words. *Not only am I able to raise a lion cub, I'm also getting to name him as well!*

"It has to be something amazing!" William thought for a few moments. However, try as he might, every name he came up with didn't seem suitable for such a magnificent creature.

"The only names I know are boring ones," William announced, clearly disappointed by his limited knowledge of names. "George, I think you should choose!"

Clearly overwhelmed by the suggestion, George gulped.

"Are you sure you want to give me this honour?"

"I am sure, George," William announced, quite relieved that

the pressure of naming such a special cub had been lifted off him. "Besides, do you really want a child of God to be named Matthew or some other boring name like that?" William's amusing explanation made both George and his father erupt with laughter.

Eventually, George seemed set on a name. William could see that this meant a lot to George, and William felt quite proud that he had made his father's friend so happy. After a quick nod to himself, a trait William shared when he needed a little self assurance, George put his suggestion forward.

"Well, you remember that wise old man I spoke of earlier, who first told me about the white lions? I met him when I was very young indeed, younger than you are now William." George nodded at William. "He lived on the outskirts of Anga. He was a very wise man and all of the villagers respected him greatly. Every so often, he would sit beside a fire and the entire village would gather around as he recounted extravagant tales from his life. We all listened, entranced by his stories. To cut a long story very short, he would always tell us that white lions were the most powerful animals in the whole of Africa, using the word "*matimba*" to describe them. So, if you don't mind, I thought we could call him Matimba?"

"Matimba! I think it is perfect!" William replied, clearly happy with the suggestion. Looking down into the bucket, William stroked the sleeping cub and whispered, "Do you hear that? You are now called Matimba, the *Great White Lion of Anga Farm*."

CHAPTER SEVEN

William spent a further hour just watching the white lion cub sleeping, clearly besotted with the new arrival. However, William's father soon felt that it was time William got some rest, reassuring his son that he would wake him in four hours for the next feeding session. After much persuasion, William finally relented and went to his bedroom.

Just as his father began to make his way back into the kitchen, William appeared once again in the sitting room, duvet and pillow in hand. Before his father had a chance to protest, William sat in the chair next to the bucket containing Matimba and positioned himself comfortably, resting his head against the pillow and wrapping himself up in his duvet.
"If I am going to rest, I want Matimba to know I am close by," William replied, aware of his father's bemusement.

Deciding that it was easier to just leave his son there, William's father made his way through to the kitchen where George had made the pair a cup of tea. Snuggled up in his duvet, William had closed his eyes. However, this was all just an act! William was just trying to convince his father that he was asleep. Before too long, his father would go to bed, then William would be able to look at Matimba for as long as he wished.

However, William's eyes soon started to feel extremely heavy and, despite his best efforts, he could not find the strength to open them. The whole experience had taken its toll on William and it was not long before he had fallen asleep in his father's chair.

William looked up and was faced by a pale lion which, like before, was glaring manically at him. The pale lion growled at the sight of William and took a single step forward, opening its mouth and bearing its large canines. This time though, William knew it was not just a pale lion. Rather, it was a white lion! Overcome by excitement, William ran towards the lion. Immediately, he knew this was a mistake. The white lion's eyes were once again full of rage and it bounded towards William, roaring furiously at him. William was frozen to the spot with fear. Petrified, he turned his head in every direction, frantically looking for help or for an escape route, only to be faced with nothing but darkness at every turn. Looking ahead again, William saw that the white lion was only a few metres away now. It lowered its head and shoulders. William noticed that its eyes had turned bright blue, and they burned with hatred. William wanted desperately to wake up but, as hard as he tried, he could not! The white lion leaped into the air, roaring so loudly it felt as if William's head was going to explode. With his ears ringing from the volume of the lion's roar, William focussed on its menacing paws which it had pulled back, ready to swipe at him. The white lion's claws were protracted and sparkled in the darkness. William closed his eyes, ready for the pain.

"This will be different though my friend." A mumbled voice from the kitchen woke William from his nightmare. Sweat ran down both sides of William's forehead, and he struggled to catch his breath. Exhausted, William lay his head back down against the chair and closed his eyes, trying to convince himself that it was just another silly dream and that he needed to calm down. After a few moments, William had got his breath back and he wiped the sweat from his brow with the corner of his duvet. As he pulled the duvet away from his face, he opened his eyes and caught a glimpse of his father and George sat at the kitchen table, talking seriously to one another.

"I know, I know!" replied one of the two. William was still exhausted and his body was telling him to go back to sleep. William's eyes became heavy and his father and George became blurred outlines, impossible to distinguish from one another.

"But what can we do? We must treat it like every other animal at the farm," one of the two men exclaimed.

Despite wanting to stay awake to find out what the pair were talking about, William's eyes were becoming far too heavy for him to keep open. Ever so slowly, his eyelids began to close again. William finally succumbed to exhaustion and fell back asleep!

"The cub's future is sealed, and it happens to be an extremely lucrative one," William's father stated.

"If this gets out, Michael, people will come! Film crews,

photographers, people from all around the world. They will come!" George replied, obviously concerned.

"Well then, we have to keep it a secret so that nobody finds out, until the time is right. Two or maybe three years," William's father exclaimed.

"What about the boy?" George said, nodding over in William's direction. "You know he has already fallen head over heels for the cub. What are you going to tell him when the time comes?"

"Don't worry." William's father looked over into the sitting room to see his son, sleeping soundly in his father's favourite chair. "I'll take care of it."

CHAPTER EIGHT

During the first few weeks that followed the birth of Matimba, William worked tirelessly to try and manage both his chores on the farm, and his role of caring for the new-born lion cub. William now had little time to spare for anything other than work. No longer did he have the time to dream about going to school. No longer did he have the time to stand by the giraffes' enclosure and watch The Twins feed, marvelling at their beauty. No longer did he have the time to play silly, childish games with Saba. William had even stopped saying "hello" to all the animals every morning. Instead, he spent this time preparing Matimba's first feed, then rushing out of the farmhouse door to get started on his next chore. Even when Matimba did not require feeding as often, William's workload did not lessen as his father would give him even more chores to compensate for the change in the cub's feeding timetable.

Despite the increase in his workload around the farm, William treasured every moment that he was able to spend with Matimba. William would race through every chore his father gave him, eager to pass the time until the next feeding session so he could see Matimba again. Every moment he spent away from Matimba now felt like wasted time to William. Even cleaning out the grazing animals, which William used to love, had now become a chore to him. William now simply cleaned out their enclosures without paying much attention to the occupants. All his energy was focussed on getting through his work so he could get back to Matimba as soon as possible. At every opportunity, William would also beg George to tell him more old folk stories about the *White Lions of Timbavati*. Be it in his father's chair with Matimba sleeping on his lap, or as the pair prepared the meat for the lions and hyenas, William would hang on every word that George uttered.

However, William also began to worry more and more about what the future held for Matimba. Over the years, William had come to accept his father's explanation for why the animals on Anga Farm could not stay there forever – this was how his father provided for William and for George's family. *But what about Matimba? Was his fate the same as all the other animals that had been taken away from the farm*? William would lay awake and ponder these questions for hours. The more time he spent with Matimba, the more he felt like a part of his life had been repaired. William never talked to anyone about the effect his mother's death had on him, not even his own father. However, he had always felt like a piece of him was missing. In the weeks that followed the birth of Matimba, William felt as though the emptiness which his mother's death had left was being filled. The thought of Matimba being taken away from him caused his eyes to fill up with tears, as he lay on his bed, alone at night.

Eventually, William could not take it any longer. One evening, when William had finished his daily chores around the farm and had fed Matimba, he walked into the kitchen where his father sat eating. After sitting himself down opposite his father, William started to fiddle nervously with a fork which had been left out on the table. Minutes passed, and William still could not bring himself to ask his father what he was planning to do with Matimba. The older William had got, the more he struggled starting conversations with his father. William just never knew what to say or how to begin!
"What do you want?" William's father asked, obviously sensing his son's anxiety from across the table.
"Well, I was just wondering," William replied nervously, "whether you were planning to sell Matimba when he gets older, like you say you have to with the other animals?" William exhaled heavily, obviously relieved to have got this off his chest at last. Looking up, William was disappointed to see that his father had just continued eating, as if William had not even spoken.

Seconds of silence passed by before William's father finally answered, "Why?"
"It's just that..." William shifted nervously in his chair and wiped the sweat from his forehead. "I don't want you to sell him." William could not think of any other way to say it. It was true. He did not want his father to sell Matimba. Once again, his father seemed to wait a lifetime to respond.
"I will **not** be selling Matimba." William's father looked back down and started to eat again. "He's worth far more than that to me."

Then there was silence. William waited for what felt like an

eternity, half expecting his father to add something further to what he had said, but he said nothing.
"Thank you," was all William could muster, before getting out of his chair and making his way back to his bedroom.

Out of sight, William punched the air in delight! His father was not going to sell Matimba after all! William could not believe it! In his bedroom, William closed the door behind him and started to bounce up and down on his bed with joy. He felt like shouting, screaming and singing all at once! He would not be losing Matimba like all the other animals!
"Keep it down in there!" William's father bellowed from the kitchen. Immediately, William got into bed and hid himself under the duvet. William was just grateful that his father had decided not to sell Matimba – he did not want to push his luck!

Before William knew it, two months had passed since the birth of Matimba and the white lion had developed into a mischievous little cub. Matimba had recently gained full control of his eyes and, consequently, his confidence had increased, as had his thirst for adventure! On several occasions, at the end of a hard day's work, William and his father would wander back into the farmhouse, ready for a well-earned meal, only to find half-eaten cushions and scratched tables flung over in the sitting room, shattered pieces of pottery littering the kitchen floor, or the shredded remnants of clothing scattered all over their bedrooms! On other occasions, William and his father would put on their work boots only to find their laces chewed to shreds, the leather ripped or, even worse, that Matimba had left a *little present* for them inside one of their boots! On some days,

William would go to the bathroom, only to find Matimba already in there, drinking water droplets from the leaking washbasin tap. Even though Saba and William had started taking Matimba on short trips out of the house and into the farm's courtyard, this seemed to do little to curb the young cub's enthusiasm for causing mischief.

On one nerve racking day in particular, William turned around to find Matimba sprinting across the courtyard towards the main lion enclosures. Luckily, Saba managed to catch the little white cub before he got too close to an enclosure housing a boisterous pair of male lions. They would have been only too happy to meet (and probably eat) the new addition to Anga Farm!

Unsurprisingly, William's father eventually ran out of patience with Matimba's antics and moved him back into the small enclosure in which he was born. The enclosure had remained empty since Bahiya had given birth to the white lion cub, so William's father thought it was the perfect place for Matimba to get used to the sights and sounds of the farm, without him getting too close to any of its occupants. While William knew that he would miss Matimba being in the farmhouse, he agreed with his father that it would be a good idea for the young white lion cub to start living outside. William was actually surprised his father had not suggested it earlier considering the damage Matimba had caused around the farmhouse!

CHAPTER NINE

It was mid-afternoon and all the occupants at Anga Farm were baking in the glorious sunshine. Outside the two smaller enclosures, William sat cross-legged on the ground. Six months had passed since Matimba had been placed in one of the enclosures by William's father, and life on the farm was beginning to get back to a relatively normal state. William's working day had become less frantic as Matimba now only required one feed a day. William gave this to Matimba alongside his father or George when they fed the other lions on the farm. In fact, William's life was starting to get back to how it used to be before Matimba had been born. William was spending more time with Saba again, and he didn't rush through every single chore that his father gave him anymore. Instead, William had come to the conclusion that, the quicker he completed his chores, the more his father gave him and, whether he rushed them or not, he still got the same number of breaks to visit Matimba. At this point in time, William was on such a break.

Inside the enclosure, the eight month old Matimba was lying

on the concrete flooring, munching happily on a juicy piece of beef which William had fed to him half an hour ago. Even though life at Anga Farm was beginning to get back to normality, one thing that William still loved to do was to just watch Matimba. For William, it didn't even matter what the white lion cub was doing. He would still be as captivated as he was the first time he had laid eyes on Matimba! Today was no different. Despite the fact that Matimba's entire muzzle was covered in blood from chomping on his food, William still thought that the lion looked spectacular. In the eight months that had passed since his birth, Matimba's glow had not diminished in anyway and the cub still looked as white as freshly fallen snow. The lifeless colour of the concrete floor and back walls in Matimba's enclosure only served to illuminate the colour of his fur and, if it were not for the steel fencing which ran across the front of his enclosure, any visitor who entered the farm and walked over to inspect the other lion enclosures would immediately see Matimba.

William watched Matimba closely as the lion held the piece of meat in his paws whilst he ripped chunks out of it, only stopping occasionally to lick the piece as well - something which always made William laugh. In the background, William could just hear the faint sound of his father shouting. Without looking back to check whether his father might want him, William carried on watching Matimba, assuming that his father would just be shouting for George, or perhaps at one of the lions in the main enclosures that had decided to steal his spade again!

Matimba sluggishly rose to his feet, stretched rather over-enthusiastically and headed over towards the water trough at the opposite end of his enclosure, trailing strands of straw from his back paw as he moved. As Matimba noisily lapped up water from the trough, William smiled as the cub's tail wafted in the air, showing Matimba's obvious pleasure at having a drink. The tip of the cub's tail had developed into a small tuft, which Matimba proudly swatted against anyone who entered his enclosure, perhaps just to show off how much he had grown. However, this was not the only change William had noticed. Matimba had also become more muscular, particularly in his shoulders, and a slight ruff of fur had started to appear under the cub's neck.

"The start of a great mane!" William mimicked George to himself. George had probably been just as excited as William to see the first few hairs beginning to develop on Matimba's neck. As William spoke, Matimba peered up from the trough. Every day, Matimba's eyes seemed to get even bluer and, against their white background, they stood out like a pair of sapphire gems. Matimba quickly lost interest in William, and returned to his water trough, obviously having yet to fully quench his thirst.

"Michael! Michael!" Immediately, William turned around. George's panicked voice shot out across the farm, and several of the animals replied aggressively with "*snarls*" and "*grunts*." William turned back around to see Matimba running into the birthing den, obviously frightened by all of the noise.
"Michael!" Once again, George shouted out, causing William to turn back around. At first, William could not see George from where he was stood. However, after taking a few steps forwards, William was able to see beyond the main lion enclosures. George came into view and William watched him

bolt across the courtyard towards the rhino enclosure, where William's father was stood, spade in hand. Wondering what all the commotion was about, William watched as the pair exchanged a brief conversation. After a few seconds, William's father dropped the spade and both he and George made their way hurriedly over towards the farmhouse. William decided that he had to find out what was going on.

With some haste, William started to make his way over to the farmhouse, which his father and George had entered just a few moments earlier. William suddenly slowed down as he heard raised voices. As William tiptoed closer to the farmhouse, he noticed that the voices were becoming louder and louder.

"What are you talking about?" William froze to the spot, as he could finally make out what was being said. William immediately recognised his father's voice, but was confused as to what had made him so angry. Edging further forwards, William strained to hear what else was being said. William heard an animated reply, but the voice was muffled so he could not make out the words. Cautiously, William tiptoed further forwards. Taking great care not to be heard, William edged up the steps onto the porch. With every step, William could hear the muffled voices a little more. He had to find out why they were so angry. Carefully, William opened the back door and stepped into the farm's kitchen.

"I have absolutely no idea what you are talking about!" William recognised his father's sharp voice once again.

"Stop pretending that you don't have one! We know you have one!"

Immediately, William realised that the muffled voice that he

hadn't been able to recognise before was in fact a woman. As she continued, William tiptoed his way through the kitchen and into the sitting room, where he hid behind his father's favourite chair. William was now only a few feet away from all the commotion.
"You have a white lion! We have it from a reliable source that you have a white lion here!" The woman's voice quivered with anger, trailing off towards the end of her accusation. William had never heard anyone as upset as the woman at the farm's front door.
"First of all, little girl, we do not have a white lion. Second of all, is it any of your business anyway?"

William was stunned. Even though he instantly knew who had said these words, he could not believe it was George. William had never heard George speak so aggressively before. *George never got angry* he thought. On the contrary, George was the happiest, kindest man William had ever met. *Why on earth was he so angry?* William thought to himself, and *how on earth did the woman find out about Matimba?*
"I know exactly what you do to animals on this farm!" The woman was now getting more and more agitated with every word she spoke. "If you have a white lion, then you have an obligation to release it! A moral obligation! All around the world, they're caged in concrete cells so tourists can gawp at them and pet them, whilst people like **you**..." the woman was now screeching with fury..."can make money out of their suffering!" From behind the chair, William could hear the woman breathing deeply, obviously exhausted with anger.

Even though William could not see her, just hearing the woman so upset made the hairs on his arms stand up on end.

Then there was silence. After a few moments, the fiercely charged atmosphere was broken when someone started clapping, followed by a sarcastic chuckle.
"Are you finished, woman?" William's father sounded as if he had found the whole episode funny. William was shocked by how rude his father came across! *How could he treat somebody like that?* William thought to himself.
"That was some speech. Truly heartfelt!" William's father continued. "However, I am afraid that you have absolutely no idea what we do on this farm and, if you had just a small idea, you would know that we do not have a white lion!"

William was shocked and utterly confused. *Why is he denying that Matimba exists and why doesn't he just let the woman come and see him?* William couldn't understand why not! *It was obvious that she cared for white lions and, when she saw how happy Matimba was, then she would leave knowing that they were caring for him well,* he thought. *George had always said they were magical creatures*, thought William. *He never mentioned anything about them being locked up for tourists to look at.* William suddenly panicked. *Was this what my father was planning to do instead of selling him? Locking him up so tourists could pay to look at him and pet him. Surely not!* William tried to reassure himself. *My father never lets anyone visit the farm that he does not know. There was no way he would allow tourists to start coming.* As William calmed down, he also wondered what on earth the woman meant when she said "I know what you do to animals on this farm!"

"I suggest you leave!" Once again, the tone of George's voice shocked William. *Why was he so angry with this woman?*
"I am going to do **everything** I can to stop you from…" The woman was cut short by the slamming of the farmhouse's

front door. William held his breath tightly, hoping that his father and George did not know he was there. William was trembling. He knew that if his father found him hiding, he would be furious!

The silence was finally broken by William's father.
"How do you think they found out?" William's father sounded livid.
"I hope you're not thinking it was me!" George replied defensively. "Why on earth would I…"
"Of course I don't think it was you George!" William's father scoffed at the thought. "We have known each other for too long. I know it wasn't you."
"William or Saba?" George's response shocked William. *How could George think I would tell anyone about Matimba?* William thought back to the promise he made his father when Matimba was born not to tell anyone about the white lion cub. *What about Saba though? What if she had told a friend? No,* William reassured himself. *She spent most days at the farm anyway! There was no way she would ever tell anyone!*
"No, don't be daft. William and Saba would never tell anyone. They're too loyal for that." His father's confidence in him made William smile a little.
"Maybe someone has broken into the farm, at night possibly?" George suggested. "They could have jumped the perimeter fencing using a ladder. They might have wanted to steal something, or maybe they were just curious. But if they saw a white lion, they would almost certainly tell someone?"
"Sounds the most likely cause," exclaimed William's father.

William's father and George had both calmed down now that the woman had left. William froze as the pair walked past the chair that he was hiding behind.

"We will have to work some night shifts, as well as checking the fencing to see if anyone has climbed over and…" His father's voice trailed off as the pair walked through the kitchen and outside onto the porch. As soon as William heard the back door shut, he finally let out an enormous breath.

"William!" Before William had time to digest what had just happened, he heard his father calling for him outside. It was obviously time to get back to work.

CHAPTER TEN

It was not long before William's father and George seemed to have forgotten the incident involving the mysterious female visitor. William had decided not to ask his father or George about it, and neither did they mention it to him. The only thing that changed following her visit was that William's father insisted that the perimeter fences be checked at the end of their working day, just before George and Saba left the farm to go home. For a few weeks, the trio would walk along the perimeter fence, looking for any signs of forced entry. However, even this soon stopped as William's father seemed to lose interest in the matter.

In the days that followed the woman's visit, William would lay on his bed, wondering who she was and what on earth she meant when she said, "I know what you do to animals on this farm." *What did she think they did at the farm?* William constantly asked himself. It had taken a while, but William had accepted his father's explanation that Anga Farm sells its animals in order to make money. Whilst he did not necessarily agree with it, and whilst he still did not have the courage to be on the farm when the animals were being taken away by their new owners, he had accepted it as part of life. *Why was the woman so angry about this?*

Eventually, William realised that there was no way he would ever find the answers to his many questions. It was not even as if he knew who the mystery woman was. He did not even see her face and he most certainly did not recognise her voice. The only women William ever met were through his trips from the farm down to George's house, and the majority of these were either George's friends or market sellers. Eventually though, the mystery woman became only a passing thought and it was not long before William had become fully immersed in farm life again.

CHAPTER ELEVEN

Twelve months had now passed since the mysterious woman's visit, and William stood on the porch, looking out over the farm. It was another glorious day. In fact, William struggled to remember the last time it rained and, whilst he enjoyed the heat, it did mean that both he and Saba had to spend more time replenishing the animals' water supplies. However, William and Saba had done that the evening before, so he did not need to worry about that just yet.

Instead, William made his way down the porch steps and towards the two smaller enclosures to check up on Matimba. As he walked, William could hear the female black rhino snorting loudly from within her enclosure, obviously annoyed at something her plucky young son had just done. The calf had been born 16 months ago, and was now just over half the size of his mother. Like Matimba, he had an extremely mischievous streak! William chuckled and continued on towards the smaller enclosures. As he passed the main lion enclosures, he smiled at the mob of big cats, sprawled out amongst the grass. Their ability to sleep for hours during the day always amused William. In the nearest enclosure to him, a single, ageing male stalked back and forth along the perimeter fencing. Even at a distance, William could hear the lion's laboured breathing, rumbling in William's direction. A few seconds later, the lion froze in the middle of his enclosure.

Glaring across at the neighbouring enclosure, the ageing male lion began to scratch away the grass beneath him with his two hind legs. William looked at the lion's mane, which only two years ago had been dark, thick and impressive. It was now thin and tattered. As the male plodded over to a corner in his enclosure, William noticed how his eyes drooped with tiredness - the fire that raged within them only two years ago had now all but fizzled out. Settling down, the lion looked blankly at the grass beneath him before eventually closing his eyes in order to get some rest. Even the snarls coming from two adolescent lions fighting in the neighbouring enclosure no longer bothered the ageing male like it used to. Instead, the male lion just seemed happy to be getting some sleep.

Looking ahead, William noticed his father, who was crouched in the far left corner of Matimba's enclosure. As William neared the enclosure, he could see his father was replenishing Matimba's trough with fresh water - something which he insisted on doing so the white lion was used to him entering the enclosure. Outside of the enclosure, propped up against the steel fencing, was his father's shovel and dust pan, which he must have used before William arrived to clean up Matimba's enclosure. In the right hand corner of the enclosure, the now 18 month old white lion was sleeping soundly in the birthing den. The wooden den served as Matimba's refuge for when he wanted to get some peace and quiet.

Gently, William unlocked the door to the enclosure and quietly stepped inside, hoping not to disturb Matimba. Even though William tried as hard as he could not to make a single sound, Matimba's hearing was far too good and the lion inquisitively raised his head to see who or what had just disturbed him from his well earned rest. However, as soon as Matimba realised it was just William, he dropped his head back down onto his thick straw bed.
"Morning boy!" William announced as he walked over to Matimba. In front of the birthing den, William crouched down and greeted Matimba by gently patting him on the top of his rear thigh. Half asleep, the white lion responded by grumbling affectionately back - something which he had done since he was a cub.

Over the last 18 months, Matimba had appeared to grow at a relentless pace! In fact, he had now grown into an impressive adolescent male. Even William's father had noted that, in comparison to the other lions he had watched grow throughout his years running the farm, Matimba was increasing in weight and stature at an unprecedented rate.
"At this rate, he's going to outgrow every enclosure on the farm," George would exclaim whenever the subject came up.

However, it wasn't just in length and height that Matimba was ahead of his predecessors. The white lion's entire frame had become far more muscular than any other lion of the same age which William's father and George had previously seen. His shoulders and the tops of his hind legs were thick with muscle! Matimba's mane was also still growing and, whilst the majority of this growth had been under his ears, around his chin and down to his chest, the white lion did now possess a rather impressive mohawk!

"How's he been this morning?" William asked his father. No answer followed and, when William turned around, his father was nowhere to be seen. Only when William looked outside the enclosure did he see his father walking off across the courtyard and in the direction of the farm's store room.

Relations between the two had recently turned sour after William finally expressed his frustration that Matimba was still being kept in one of the two smaller enclosures. William felt that, because Matimba was nearly two years of age, he now required a larger living area and the opportunity to interact with the other lions at the farm. By having this opportunity, William believed that Matimba would be able to experience an entirely different world to the one he currently knew. Whilst, from a distance, Matimba could just about see a few of the other lions in their enclosures (and he certainly heard their territorial roars from where he was), everything he had learnt had been from William or his father. William now believed that it was time for Matimba to learn from his "own kind," and that the white lion was old enough, and strong enough, to hold his own against some of the farm's other lions. It had taken William days to pluck up the courage to tell his father this and, when he did, his father was not entirely impressed with his son's proposal.
"He's fine where he is, Will. There's nothing wrong with him!" William's father had replied, refusing to even discuss the suggestion. "Anyway, if we get any unwelcome visitors to the farm, they would easily see Matimba if he was living with

the rest of the lions. Then, who knows what might happen. Someone may even try to take him from us and then sell him! We can't let that happen!" William's father had told his son.

Whilst William knew how rare white lions were, and accepted that he would not know what to do if somebody did try and take Matimba away from him, he still could not help but feel frustrated. Deep down, William knew that his father was probably just thinking about what was best for Matimba and that it was important for the white lion's safety to keep him out of view, but William believed that it was worth taking the chance. William could not help but think that, if Matimba was able to talk to them, he would want them to move him as well. At the time, William was almost bursting with frustration. All he wanted was the very best for Matimba.

William had always been too scared to challenge his father's decisions, but this time it was different. William felt a deep responsibility for the well-being of Matimba and he wanted to know that he had done everything he could for the white lion. Despite this, William and his father were both shocked when suddenly, out of nowhere, William challenged his father's decision.

"But it's not fair! Matimba deserves to be with the other lions! I know it's what he wants." It had taken a few moments for his father to believe that William had actually dared to question a decision of his.

"I beg your pardon boy!" His father's voice thundered! William had been frozen to the spot with fear. The hairs on his arms had stood on end, his back stiffened and his mouth became dry. William's father simply glared at his son, without saying a single word. William knew that he had made a mistake. Never had William questioned his father's authority, always too frightened of the consequences that it would lead to. Standing only a few metres away, it was clear that William's father was furious! Seconds passed by, yet he continued to glare at his son. Eventually, without saying a single word, William's father had turned away and stormed out of the farmhouse.

Throughout the days that had followed their conversation, William's father had said little to his son, only speaking when he wanted William to do a specific chore. In fact, William's father did his best to keep away from his son at all times, purposefully eating at different points in the day to William, working late on the farm and frequently disappearing without giving any clue as to where he was going. Despite this, William felt little guilt over what he had done. He had stood up for what he believed was right for Matimba and he was proud of himself for doing so. However, he had little hope that it was actually going to make any difference.

Back in the enclosure, William decided it was time he got on with his chores, starting off with cleaning the eland enclosure. Unsurprisingly, Matimba had fallen asleep some time ago. On the rare occasions when Matimba was awake, William would normally say goodbye to his friend by patting him on the side, scratching behind his ear and under his chin or running his fingers gently through the white lion's tufty mane. However, he did not want to wake him so he simply whispered, "See you later boy," and tiptoed out of Matimba's enclosure. After closing the door behind him, he carefully turned the key which his father had left in the lock, and started to make his way over to the farm's store room, where the cleaning equipment was kept.

"*Ring-ring, ring-ring!*" The sound of the farm's telephone startled William and, he looked over to the farmhouse in surprise. Rarely did the phone ring and, when it did, people with strange accents always asked to speak to his father. Like with most unexpected sounds on the farm, it was quickly followed by a wave of grumpy reactions from some of the farm's animals, obviously unhappy at being disturbed!

William smiled as nearly every lion on the farm ran to the edges of their enclosures and hissed, snarled or roared at the disturbance. From within their enclosure, both the female rhino and her son snorted loudly in disgust. The three hyenas seemed to find the entire episode hilarious, laughing hysterically amongst themselves and running manically up and down the edges of their enclosure.

"*Bang!*" Startled once again, William looked up. Ahead of him, his father had just shut the food preparation room door behind him and was jogging across the courtyard in the direction of the farmhouse.

"*Ring-ring, ring-ring*!" The phone continued as William's father increased his speed, obviously trying to reach the phone in time. Without acknowledging him, William's father passed his son in the middle of the courtyard and jogged up the porch steps and through the farm's back door.

"*Ring-ring, ring-ring*!"

As William continued to make his way over to the store

room, he noticed Saba to his left, standing in front of the eland enclosure, watching its occupants munching happily on the grass beneath them.

"She loves those eland!" Taken by surprise by the deep voice in his ear, William let out a high pitched shriek. Behind him, George started chuckling to himself, obviously amused at William's reaction. Unlike Saba, George was actually very good at sneaking up on people without being detected, and this was not the first time that he had done this to William.

"I'm sorry Will, but I could not resist!" Still smiling to himself, George placed an arm around William's shoulders and they both looked over at Saba, who was reaching into the eland enclosure and scratching the head of a bulky male as he eagerly munched on the grass beneath his hooves. George seemed relatively at ease, despite the fact that his daughter was stroking the male, with her fingers only a matter of centimetres away from his two enormous, swirling horns!

"I don't think she is happier than when she is here with these animals." As he spoke, George looked around the farm, as if to reinforce his point.

"I know," William agreed but, before he could continue, his father suddenly burst out of the farm's back door and looked around. As soon as he saw George, he waved him over.

"I think I am wanted," George sighed as he patted William on the shoulder and started to walk towards the farmhouse.

Laughing to himself, William decided to go over and ask Saba if she wanted to help him clean out the eland enclosure. Eland were one of the few animals on the farm that paid neither William nor Saba any attention when the pair cleaned out their enclosure. Even on the occasions when William or Saba made loud noises through talking, laughing or clumsily dropping things such as a shovel, the eland would always look up at the pair, show their disapproval and quickly return to eating, sleeping or simply continuing to stare into space.

As William walked over towards Saba, who was still completely engrossed with the male eland, William noticed his father making his way down the porch steps in order to meet George in the middle of the courtyard. When the pair came together, they were just within hearing distance of William, who had yet to reach Saba.
"We need to move him to the paddock - right away!" William's father announced. After a short conversation with George, the pair began to make their way towards the paddock. William's back stiffened and the hairs on his arms stood on end at the very mention of the paddock. Even though this had happened on numerous occasions before, William always felt the same sudden rush of anxiety when he heard that an animal was being put in the paddock. Sweat began to pour down William's brow and his heart began to pound heavily in his chest as he considered, just for a second, that Matimba might be the one being moved to the paddock.

"Will! Come here!" William gasped out loud, clearly startled by the sound of his father's voice. William turned to face his father but, before he could reply, the sound of a door slamming caused William to look to his left. In the distance, outside the farm's store room door, George was standing with a brown collar and a metal chain in one hand, and a fire extinguisher in the other. William's heart sank as it dawned on him that it was a lion that was being taken away.

"Matimba is not being taken is he? You promised me that he

was too valuable to sell!" William bellowed in horror at his father. William could not contain his anguish at the thought of losing his best friend. Taken slightly aback by his son's outburst, William's father stuttered slightly before finally replying.
"No Will! Matimba is staying exactly where he is. But there's this zoo owner from America. He is only in town for today! He says he's after a lion, a male lion, for his zoo. Apparently, he was meant to have a lion from somewhere down south, but they cancelled on him. So, he's coming up later today to have a look at the Big Fella.

The Big Fella was the 11 year old male lion that William had passed earlier in the day, labouring around in his enclosure. The ageing lion had arrived at Anga Farm as a new-born cub, only a few days old and not long after William himself had been born. Whilst on a business trip in Johannesburg, William's father had heard about a lioness which had recently given birth to a cub at a well known circus. The lioness had spent all of her life travelling through Africa and the rest of the world and was regarded as the circus' star attraction. The circus, even though extremely popular whenever it came to Johannesburg, had a reputation for severely neglecting the animals in its care.

William's father had heard of animals being kept in small, poorly constructed cages, rarely being fed and, on some occasions, even beaten as a way to encourage them to perform new, *entertaining* tricks. However, the circus had recently started to lose trade and had therefore begun to make cut-backs to save money. The last thing the circus wanted was the financial burden of a cub. William's father decided to pay the circus a visit and, after brief negotiations, managed to persuade the owner to sell the cub at a reasonable price. From then on, William's father had hand-reared the cub, much like he and William did with Matimba, and it was not long before the cub had matured into a magnificent male lion with a thick, dark mane and an earth-rumbling roar. The male had also gone onto father many of the lions which currently lived on the farm and he was, in fact, Matimba's father.

Unfortunately, the male lion was no longer the same magnificent specimen that he had once been. Those glory days were now sadly behind him, and the male was beginning to show his age. Like many of the animals before him at Anga Farm, the male lion had become frail and his health had started to deteriorate. The time for the male lion to leave the farm had finally arrived.

William had known the Big Fella all his life. He had watched him transform into a magnificent, mature male lion who oozed confidence and struck fear in the occupants of his neighbouring enclosures. On one hand, William could not help but feel relieved that it was not Matimba that his father was prepared to sell but, on the other hand, William could not hide his deep sadness that he was never going to see the old lion again. Even though it did not come as a huge surprise to William that the Big Fella was being sold, he had spent every day of his life walking past the Big Fella's enclosure and, from tomorrow onwards, he would no longer be there. At that moment, tears began to run down the sides of William's face, as he imagined life at the farm without the Big Fella.

"You don't have to be here so you do not have to worry about that." His father's caring tone surprised William. William was also relieved that he would not have to be on the farm when they took the Big Fella away. Just knowing that the lion was leaving was too much for William. To actually see him being taken away would be unthinkable.
"Also, I'll make sure our visitor doesn't know Matimba is here," his father continued. "You don't have to worry about that either. Matimba's enclosure is far away from the paddock and our visitor will have no reason to look around the farm…he is here only for one thing."

William's father suddenly became silent and he looked blankly over William's right shoulder. Unsure of what to do, William considered asking his father whether he was feeling alright. William even looked over his own shoulder to try and figure out what his father was looking at, only to find nothing out of the ordinary behind him. Looking back at his father, William started to become concerned yet, before he had chance to say anything, his father blinked several times and glanced up at his son.
"Anyway, I need George here with me today to help move the Big Fella, so you will have to go to his house without him and you'll need to take Saba with you as well. You should know the route by now and I think it will do you good." William's father made sure to raise his voice when he mentioned Saba's name and, for the first time throughout their whole conversation, she actually looked away from the male eland and noticed the pair.
"What's that?" she exclaimed, bewildered by the attention she was getting from both William and his father.
"William will explain to you, Saba, but count yourself lucky. It

means you won't have to clean out the zebras today!" Just for a moment, William's father let out a short laugh at the sight of Saba's gleaming face. As William looked at his father, who was still smiling at Saba's delighted expression, he struggled to remember the last time he had heard the sound of his father laughing.
"Get your things together. You will stay over at George's tonight and he will bring you back tomorrow when we are done here," he told William.

William's father started to make his way over towards the Big Fella's enclosure then, after just a few steps, he stopped and slowly turned around to face his son. Lifting his finger and pointing it directly at his son, William's father shouted.
"One last thing Will – make sure you look after her!" He moved his finger to point in Saba's direction, who suddenly looked bemused that someone would think she was not capable of looking after herself. Confused, Saba replied.
"What's that supposed to mean?" With her arms stretched out wide in front of her, Saba waited patiently for either William, or his father, to reply. Instead, they both walked off in opposite directions, leaving the young girl all by herself, still wondering why on earth she needed someone to look after her!

It took only a few minutes for William to grab some essential items for his stop-over at Saba's house. Frantically, he had raced around his bedroom, picking up random pieces of clothing without giving them much thought whatsoever. In fact, William just wanted to get off the farm as soon as he could. There was no way that he wanted to be around when the American turned up, and he did not want to be there to

see the Big Fella being moved from his enclosure to the paddock either. Bursting through the kitchen door and clearing the porch steps with a single leap, William threw his backpack over his shoulder and called over to Saba.
"Saba, I'm ready! Let's go!"

However, Saba was in no rush at all. Ignoring William's flustered instruction, Saba simply continued to stroke the male eland through the fence, completely unaware of William's strong desire to leave the farm as soon as possible. It wasn't until William had jogged over to the eland enclosure and startled the male by loudly clapping his hands that Saba finally rose to her feet in frustration.
"Why did you do that?" Saba cried out as the distressed male ran away to the other side of the enclosure. "Look! You've upset him now!"
"I'm sorry, but you weren't listening to me! We have to leave right now!" William insisted as he turned away from Saba and began to make his way over to the farm's gate.
"Ok, don't get yourself all worked up!" Saba replied, as she patted the mud off her knees. For just a moment, Saba petulantly refused to follow William, not wanting him to think that she was impressed by what he had just done. However, it was not long before Saba became restless stood on her own. She soon decided that it was not worth the boredom, so she sprinted after William, who was now impatiently waiting for her beside the farm's gate.

In comparison to William, Saba had never become overly upset whenever she discovered that one of the animals was set to leave the farm. Years ago, when Saba's mother had secured herself a new job, George knew he was going to have

to bring his daughter to work everyday. Consequently, George quickly realised that he would have to explain to Saba that not all of the animals could stay at the farm forever. Knowing his daughter's inquisitive nature, George realised that it would not be too long before she started asking questions about why some of the animals would suddenly disappear without warning. Rather than make up some childish explanation, George decided that the best strategy was to tell Saba that the animals needed to be sold for the farm to make money. In comparison to William, Saba seemed to understand why William's father had to occasionally sell one of animals at the farm. Whenever William would try to share his anxieties with Saba about the animals leaving, she would always respond nonchalantly.
"It's not like they're dying, is it Will? I bet they've got an even better life at their new home, with even bigger enclosures and even more food to eat."

William always found it very difficult to share Saba's optimism! He could never explain it but, deep down, William always had a bad feeling about where the animals were going.
"You need to trust your father more," Saba would tell William. "He wouldn't sell an animal to anyone who would hurt them, would he?" Again, for some unknown reason which he could never explain, William just could not share Saba's optimism.

During these discussions, Saba would also point out to William that her father's job probably relied on the money the farm made from selling the occasional animal.
"What would we do if your father magically stopped selling animals?" Saba would fiercely say to William. "Our family

cannot survive on what my mother earns alone. Unlike our neighbours, my family can afford to eat properly because of what your father does!" Every time Saba argued this point, William would always become quiet and lost in his own thoughts. Part of him would regret even suggesting that his father should stop. He knew the importance of George's job to Saba's family and he would never ever want her family to go hungry. William wondered whether he was actually being selfish whenever he questioned his father's motives for selling the animals at the farm. However, no matter what William thought about how his father made money and whether he agreed with Saba's arguments or not, William could never envisage a day where he would be able to help his father move an animal to the paddock, or help to lure it into a container to then be driven away by some stranger.

I'd better get used to walking this journey then, William thought as he untied the flimsy piece of rope which barely managed to keep the farm's gate shut. After opening the gate wide enough to allow both himself and Saba to squeeze through, he gently pushed it back and re-tied the rope. Once William was satisfied that he had tied the rope tightly enough, William looked over towards the main group of lion enclosures in the distance. He envisioned Matimba, just behind them and out of view in one of the smaller enclosures, sleeping soundly without a care in the world, his giant paws hanging motionlessly in the air, twitching occasionally when something exciting was happening in one of his dreams.
"See you soon Matimba," William whispered to himself.

"Are you actually talking to yourself?" William turned around to find Saba staring at him in disbelief. "I swear you are getting weirder and weirder by the day!"

William could not help but laugh out loud when he saw the look on Saba's face. But, rather than waste any more time by arguing with her, William just wanted to get as far away from the farm as he could.
"When I first met you, I thought *God,* he's strange! But now, you're even stranger…" Saba continued her verbal assault on William as she started to make her way down the track which led away from the farm.

William had stopped listening to Saba, and was instead imagining the strange American who his father spoke of, probably making his way to the farm right now in order to collect his latest purchase - the Big Fella. As William walked beside Saba, he just hoped that she was right and that the American would show the same love and compassion to the Big Fella that both William and his father had shown to him throughout his life on the farm.

CHAPTER TWELVE

The people of Anga were familiar with the searing temperatures which often thwarted their attempts to complete the most basic of tasks. Even walking became hazardous in this weather, as dehydration posed a genuine threat. As William looked up into the sky, there was not a single cloud for miles! As a result, very few locals had dared to venture out and the main track into Anga was practically empty. Even the market traders, who rarely gave up any opportunity to try and make some money, had not attempted to pitch their stalls!

It was not long after William and Saba had set out on their journey that both their brows and backs were soaking and they were quenching their thirst on the water which William had thankfully remembered to pack at the last minute. Even though the journey to Saba's house was relatively short - just over an hour - William and Saba were still suffering from the soaring heat and, on several occasions, they both seriously considered turning back. However, for William, the thought of what lay in store back at the farm caused him to successfully persuade Saba to continue on each occasion that she demanded that they return.

As the pair took a short break to take refuge from the heat under a small acacia tree, William spotted a solitary vulture in the sky. The creature soared majestically, appearing as if it did not have a single care in the world! William loved all animals and, for some reason, he also loved vultures! Every time one decided to visit the farm, either by landing on the porch or the gate, William always found their gaze threatening, yet spellbinding. William hated it when Saba said that they were "ugly." Whilst a part of William understood what Saba meant by this, William thought that they had a special aura about them which deserved respect. As the solitary vulture continued on its journey out into the remotest regions of the bush, William wondered what it was like out there and what the vulture would be passing as it glided overhead.

Even though his father had told William that they had regularly gone on long walks into the bush together when William was a young boy, William had no memory of this whatsoever. This was not for the want of trying either. William would spend hours on his bed at night, trying desperately to recall some long lost memory of what it must have been like out there. The only images that he ever had were from the various tales that Saba had fascinated him with from her own experiences. Saba often recited tales of watching wild lions whilst they fed on a carcass, fighting bitterly with one another over the tiniest of morsels. She spoke of seeing rhinos furiously charging at cars which dared to approach them and of elephants using their sheer power to tear down entire trees with only their trunks! William had never seen a wild lion and he often wondered how different they would be compared to the lions on the farm. *Would they ever accept a white lion like Matimba? Could Matimba ever fit into a wild pride? Could he ever lead his own pride, accompanied by several wild females and his own tiny cubs?*

"What you thinking about, Will?" Saba cheerfully asked as she looked over at William. The walk had done her good and, despite the energy-sapping heat, Saba was in a much better mood now. In fact, William noticed that, rather worryingly, her energy levels actually seemed to be increasing! She even ran ahead of William kicking a tiny stone into the distance; something which William had noticed that she liked to do some years ago whenever they made this trip with George.

The sound of the stone rattling along the ground was quickly drowned out by the roar of an oncoming truck from behind them. Rocking precariously from side to side, the deep pot-holes were swallowing the truck's tyres and threatening to over-turn it at any moment. The extra acceleration needed by the enormous truck to get out of these pot-holes caused plumes of dust to form behind the vehicle, which swirled around in all directions. William and Saba cleverly evaded being caught up in the cloud by hiding behind a couple of nearby bushes!

Laughing at their near-miss and feeling slightly smug with themselves at their own ingenuity, the paired waved the truck goodbye as it continued on its perilous journey down the main track and towards the town centre. Once it had disappeared, Saba suddenly looked up at William. William immediately recognised a familiar, mischievous glint in Saba's

eyes.
"Bet you can't catch me!" Saba shouted as she shoved past William and began to sprint away from him down the track.
"I'm not in the mood, Saba!" William replied, exhausted by the heat. After sprinting for a few more metres, Saba stopped, looked back over her shoulder and childishly stuck her tongue out at William, coaxing him into chasing her.
"Go on then," William muttered to himself, as he started to race after Saba. However, just as Saba had reached a sprint, she caught her front foot in the edge of a pot-hole. Instinctively, Saba threw her arms out in front of her, hoping to lessen the impact of the fall. With an almighty thud, she came crashing to the ground.
"Saba!" William cried out.

Even at a distance, William could clearly hear Saba groaning in pain. Frantically, William sprinted down the track to where Saba was lying on her side in the middle of an enormous pot-hole, covered from head to toe in sand and dirt.
"Are you alright?" William asked as he looked all over Saba for any obvious sign of injury.
"Oh, I'm doing great!" Saba managed to sarcastically mumble, as she propped herself up on her elbows. "My head hurts a bit though," Saba moaned as she rubbed her forehead.

William immediately lifted her hair and inspected her brow, only to find it smeared with blood from where she had touched it.
"Just move your hand," William said. When Saba pulled her hand away, blood immediately started to run down the side of her forehead. William tried to inspect the wound more closely without having to touch it, but it was full of sand and dirt

from the fall and he had no idea how deep or wide the cut was.
"You're bleeding," William explained as he carefully mopped some of the blood up with the cuff of his shirt, trying as best as he could not to hurt Saba.
"Owww!" Irritated, Saba smacked William on the arm. "That hurts!"
"Sorry Saba!" William took his shirt off and rolled it up into the smallest bundle he could make. He then told Saba to keep it held against her brow to help stop the bleeding.
"We need to take you back to the farm to let my father have a look at you."

Despite the amount of walking they had already done, they were still closer to the farm than they were to Saba's house, and nobody would be there to help her anyway. William did not know where Saba's mother worked, and Saba was in no fit state to show him. Even though William had wanted to get as far away from the farm as possible earlier on, he knew that this was serious and that he needed to let his father have a look at the wound on Saba's head. He also knew that, if they were quick, they could probably get back to the farm, have Saba all cleaned up and be back on their way before the American arrived. Grabbing Saba firmly by the arm, William carefully helped her up to her feet and, after a few moments of limping forwards gingerly, the pair gradually made their way back up the track and towards the farm.

Suddenly, William remembered his father's last words to him. "One last thing, Will – make sure you look after her!" Gulping heavily, William did not dare think about how angry his father was going to be with him when he saw the state

Saba was in.

CHAPTER THIRTEEN

After gently guiding Saba into his father's favourite chair, William ran to the kitchen and searched frantically through the cupboards and kitchen drawers, looking for some type of clean rag or towel that he could use to wipe Saba's brow. The journey back up to the farm had taken longer than William had initially anticipated, and Saba's forehead had not stopped bleeding yet, despite her keeping William's shirt pressed against it. After a few minutes of frenzied searching, William eventually found several rags which his father had made from tearing up an old t-shirt.

"Got one!" Relieved, William raced over to his father's chair and placed the first rag tenderly onto Saba's brow. It did not take long for the entire rag to turn red, soaking up the surface blood which had not yet dried.
"Owww!" Saba groaned at the initial pressure, but refrained from hitting William on this occasion. After a few seconds, William removed the first bloodied rag and threw it to the floor, replacing it immediately with another.
"Are you feeling ok?" William quietly asked as he continued

to press the rag against Saba's brow.
"I feel a little dizzy, but I think I'm fine." Saba had her eyes closed as she replied.

For the first time, William noticed Saba's hand shaking slightly as it lay gently on the arm of the chair. The thought of Saba in pain made William's stomach churn. He knew he had to go and get his father, and quickly.
"Hold this firmly against where it hurts," William ordered as he replaced the second bloodied rag with a new one. "I need to go and get my father to have a look at you." William quickly got up from the floor and looked down once again at Saba's hand. It was still shaking!
"Be as quick as you can." Saba's soft voice trembled as she kept the rag pressed firmly against her brow.
"I'll be as quick as I can, I promise!" Without hesitation, William ran through the kitchen and out onto the farm's porch.

As William raced down the wooden porch steps, he could not take his eyes off the black land cruiser which was parked a few feet away from the store and food-preparation building. William suddenly had a sinking feeling in his stomach! Despite his best efforts, he was too late! The American was already here! A part of William just wanted to run away! The last thing on earth that he wanted to see was the Big Fella being packaged up into a container and shipped off to a new home. However, he could not help but think of Saba, sitting all alone in the farmhouse, relying on William to get help. With that in mind, and taking in a deep breath, William sprinted across the courtyard towards to the land cruiser. Its front lights seemed to glare threateningly at William, warning him not to take a step further.

Treading quietly alongside the land cruiser, William could not help but feel dwarfed by its sheer size. William wondered if anyone was inside or around the land cruiser. *Perhaps they could help with Saba,* William thought to himself. With Saba's interests at heart, William stood up on his tiptoes and peered through the darkened passenger window, trying to see if anyone was there. On the black, leather covered front passenger seat, William could just make out what appeared to be a long, slim case which had been left opened with its contents removed. Beside it, William also noticed several pieces of paper which were neatly stacked on top of one another. Taking a few steps backwards, William inspected the land cruiser one final time. William realised that he would probably never see such an immaculate vehicle again in his lifetime.

"Saba!" William suddenly blurted out to himself. William could not believe that he had momentarily forgotten about his friend, and he looked furiously at the land cruiser, clearly annoyed that it had distracted him. William sprinted around the back of the vehicle and towards the paddock, where he assumed his father would be. With no time to lose, William ran around the store and food preparation building and came to an immediate stop. Within the paddock, the Big Fella was gnawing away at what appeared to be a half-eaten animal carcass.

William looked around in all directions, searching for his father or anyone that could help. However, there was no-one to be found! *They must be feeding him before he leaves the farm,*

William concluded, as he watched the lion continue to feast on the carcass. The sight and sound of William had not distracted the Big Fella away from his meal in anyway. In fact, the male lion simply continued to chew on the carcass before him, as if he had no idea that William was even there. Once again, William thought about Saba, sitting all alone with her brow bleeding and her hand shaking uncontrollably. William looked around, desperate to find help! William took a few more steps towards the paddock, searching frantically for his father. *He has to be here somewhere!*

All of a sudden, William saw something ahead of him move! In the centre of the paddock, behind a small cluster of bushes, the slightest of movements caught William's attention. William took a few steps forward, trying to get a better look of what it was. From where he was standing, it was difficult to see through the thick foliage. At first, it looked like some kind of dark object, hiding behind the thick coverage of the bush. William continued on forwards, trying not to make a sound.

Suddenly, he came to a halt. He peered at the mysterious object one more time, hardly believing what he was seeing. It was a person! Only a few feet away from the exterior fencing of the paddock, William could clearly make out the outline of a person! Then the silhouette moved slightly forwards, revealing two further silhouettes. Immediately, William recognised them both! It was his father and George! *What on earth are they doing?* William thought to himself! It finally dawned on William that the mysterious person must be the American! *He must be taking a closer look at the Big Fella,* William realised. Then, out of the blue, the American began to move again! This time, he lifted up his arms.

William's entire body froze! His mouth gaped open in shock! Within the bush, the American had just lifted up a rifle! William watched in complete horror as the American aimed his rifle carefully towards the Big Fella, who was still gorging himself on the carcass, completely unaware of the impending threat! William could feel the blood draining from his entire body. His heart began to pound so loudly that he thought his chest was going to explode! *He couldn't! He isn't!* William screamed in his head! William glared at his father and George. *Why are they not stopping him?* With his mouth still gaped open, William wanted to scream as loud as he could! He wanted to tell the Big Fella to hide somewhere! But nothing came out. Every time he tried, nothing came out of his mouth! The shock of what was unfolding had silenced him. As the American re-adjusted himself, tears began to run down the sides of William's cheeks.

"Bang! Bang!" Two deafening gunshots rang out. William's heart stopped! He watched in horror as the Big Fella's body spun into the air, as the American continued to unload round after round on him. *"Bang! Bang!"* William's eyes widened! In a state of disbelief, he watched the Big Fella's body as it came crashing back down to the ground.

At that moment, time seemed to stand still! Silence had engulfed the entire farm. The hyenas dipped their heads, too afraid to even make a sound. Startled, all of the other lions froze, petrified by what they had just heard! The grazers scattered in all directions within their enclosures, clambering over one another in their confined space, trying desperately to find an escape route! William blinked several times, unable to comprehend what he had just seen. In fact, he had yet to breathe since the first shot had rung out. William's mouth remained agape and his eyes were still fixed on the lifeless body only a few metres ahead of him.

"Will!" William's entire body shuddered at the sound of his father's voice. "Will! What are you…!" Without thinking, William turned around, not even daring to look at his father, and started to run as fast as he could back to the farmhouse.
"Who is that?" An unfamiliar voice cried out.
"Will!" William could now hear both his father and George shouting his name, their voices riddled with panic. Without stopping, William ignored their calls and sprinted across the courtyard. He ran faster and faster! He just wanted to get as far away from his father as possible. Arriving at the porch, William cleared the steps with a single stride, threw the back door open, almost ripping it from its hinges, and ran through the kitchen and into his bedroom. As he ran through the farmhouse, he heard Saba yell "What's going on?" William slammed his bedroom door shut.

William collapsed on the edge of his bed and started to sob! Tears poured through his shaking hands which covered his face. *How could his father do this? How could he just let that man kill his lion!* Both hate and anger began to boil inside of William as he continued to sob on the edge of his bed.

"Crash!" William's father came bursting through the bedroom door and stood just in front of his son.
"What the hell are you doing here, boy?!" William's father snarled aggressively, his face covered in sweat and his cheeks

burning red with rage. Breathing heavily, he stared down at his son, his fists clenched, waiting for a response. William's heart was beating so violently that it felt as if it was going to burst out of his chest. He was even struggling to breathe. Sweat was pouring down the sides of his face and William suddenly began to feel faint! The sight of the Big Fella's body riddled with bullets, twisting mid-air, kept running through his mind.

"Well! What are you doing here?" bellowed William's father. William could not bring himself to speak. He even opened his mouth to try and reply, but nothing came out. Again and again, the same vision played out in William's mind. The Big Fella soaring into the air from the impact of the bullets piercing into his side. His limp body crashing to the ground as the American continued to remorselessly pull the trigger.

"If you're just going to cry like a little girl, then I'll speak!" William's father shouted. "I'm afraid this is it! You now know the **real** truth! This is how we **really** make our money! This is what has put the food on our tables since your mother died! I've spent all of your life protecting you from the truth! But now you know!" The word *truth* made William's stomach churn as he finally pulled his hands away from his face. *How could he use that word? Truth! He has lied to me for years and was now talking about the truth!*

"The truth is that we are a hunting farm, Will! We let men, women, teenagers...anybody, I don't care, come from around the world to pay good money to shoot our animals!" Taking a deep breath, William's father was getting more animated with every passing moment. William still could not bring himself to look at his father. He continued to feel more and more nauseous with every single word that his father spoke. His mind raced. His vision went blurred. *How could he do this to me? How could he have lied for so long?*

"That is the truth and I have spent years trying to protect you from it, but now you know! Now you must grow up and realise that life isn't about playing with lions! It's about putting food on the table, clothes on **your** back and keeping **us** alive." By now, William's father was standing over his son and accusingly pointing down at William, as if it was William's fault that the Big Fella was now dead.

"The sooner you get used to the idea, the better! It's always been this way and it always will be!" William's father bellowed.

Sitting on the edge of his bed, William continued to sob as his father made his way over to the bedroom door. Try as he might, William could not stop the image of the Big Fella's body falling lifelessly to the ground playing over and over in his mind. The tears kept rolling down his cheeks and his forehead was still dripping with sweat. Then, all of a sudden, William's eyes widened and his mouth opened.

"Matimba!" William cried out as he rose from the edge of his bed. In the doorway, his father abruptly stopped. With his back now facing his son, William's father stood there for what seemed like an eternity to William. In a state of panic, William felt detached from his body. No longer could he feel the tears rolling down the sides of his face, or his heart pounding within his chest. All he cared about was Matimba!

"His fate is the same as the rest of them…only it's a far more lucrative fate." His father's words sliced through the air like a sword, piercing William's heart! Almost paralysed with pain, William only just managed to utter a few words.
"But you can't! He's my best friend!" With each word William could feel his heart breaking into a thousand pieces.
"Don't you ever tell me what to do again!" As he spoke, William's father rushed forwards towards William and aggressively raised his right hand. William looked up in terror! Petrified, he stumbled backwards. As his father continued towards him, William's knee clattered into the side of his bed, causing him to fall to the floor. William dared not move. He could feel the menacing shadow of his father looming over him. Paralysed with fear, William did not even dare to breathe.

"Don't you ever tell me what to do again!" his father yelled one final time. The anger in his voice had lost none of its vigour, despite William's fall. Still too terrified to look up at his father, William just closed his eyes and hoped he would leave. As William lay on the floor, he could feel both his knees and hands uncontrollably shaking. Terrified that this would incense his father even more, he quickly reached out both of his hands and pulled his knees up into his chest. William prayed as hard as he could for his father to leave.
"If you think for one moment **that** lion is any different to the rest of them out there, then you're mistaken, boy. The sooner you accept that, the better!"

For the next few moments, William's father continued to stand over his son. Neither the sound of his heavy breathing nor the tightness of his clenched fists lessened at any point.

After what seemed like an age to William, his father broke the tense silence.
"Now, make yourself useful and go and clean out the eland enclosure. I've got a client to say goodbye to." Still crouched on the floor, William still did not dare move. Instead, he continued to stare at the wooden floor-boards beneath him until he eventually heard the farm's back door slamming shut.

Still trembling, William's knees buckled every time he tried to lift himself up off the floor. With each attempt, he became increasingly frustrated and upset with himself. On the fourth attempt, he immediately froze! Whilst struggling to stand, he heard the faint sound of someone breathing outside his bedroom door. Panic-stricken and fearing his father had returned, William's whole body went numb.

"Are you ok?" A familiar voice suddenly broke through the silence. Glancing up, William was relieved to see George peering through the bedroom door at him. Shifting his weight to make himself more comfortable, William watched George approach him. Compared to the aggressive sound of his father's footsteps, George appeared to effortlessly glide through the room. Standing next to William, George held out a reassuring hand. Taking a deep breath and, after wiping his face dry, William looked down at his own right hand. It was still trembling. Embarrassed, William immediately hid it behind his back, hoping that George had not seen it.
"Take my hand," George whispered whilst giving William a gentle nod of encouragement. His smile somehow helped to relieve the tension in the room. Taking another deep breath, William eventually pulled his hand out from behind his back and placed it into George's palm. In one smooth motion,

George used all his strength to pull William up onto the bed. Despite now being seated, William's knees continued to uncontrollably shake and William again placed both his hands on top of them to try and make them stop.
"Thank you," William whispered; too frightened to speak aloud in case his father heard him.

Seconds passed without the pair saying anything to one another. William remained sat on the edge of his bed, his hands on his knees, staring at the ground. His knees and hands stopped shaking slightly and his breathing became more settled. Every so often, a tear rolled down the side of his face. William remained silent, searching for a way to understand what he had just seen and heard.
"I think I owe you an explanation," George whispered, almost embarrassed. Without waiting for a reply from William, he continued on.
"I…" Gulping heavily, George paused for a moment, trying to find the right words to use. "I haven't got a choice, William. I have a family to look after. I don't have the privilege of choosing or creating my own path in life and, if I could, please believe me when I say this is not the path I dreamt about following as a little boy."

Shaking his head with frustration, George gazed into the space before him. As William looked up at George, another tear rolled down his cheek and onto the edge of his chin, where it hung for just a moment. William reached up and wiped the tear away from his chin with his hand. As he pulled his hand back, William caught a glimpse of a small patch of dried blood on his palm, which must have come from Saba's brow only a short time ago. Thinking back to when he and

Saba had set off to walk down to the town centre, William could not believe how long ago that now seemed. Looking closely at the dried patch of blood on his palm, he could not help but think of the Big Fella and all the other animals which had been hunted for money at the farm over the years. *Why did they have to die? Why couldn't my father have thought of a different way to make a living?*

Clenching his fists, William felt a sudden rush of anger surge up through his stomach and into the back of his throat. William could no longer hide his frustration.
"But why should they die just to keep you in a job? It's not their fault!" Furiously, William pointed in the direction of the enclosures on the farm. "Why is it that you and my father have the right to decide whether they live or not? Why is it that money is more important than their right to live?" William angrily threw both his arms up into the air. Without saying anything, George just sat and listened to William, who seemed to be getting more and more frustrated with every passing moment.

"Do you remember the night when Matimba was born?" William asked George. George said nothing but simply nodded in response.
"Well, **you** told me that he was a miracle! You told me that he was the son of a God, a beacon of hope for us all. You said that you must never harm a white lion - **ever**! Are you just going to stand by and let the same thing happen to Matimba…just for money?" William again threw both of his hands up into the air in frustration. As his arms fell back down onto his lap, he took in a deep breath, then exhaled heavily. William was not used to getting angry. He felt dizzy!

Sweat was pouring down his brow again and the feeling of his blood pulsating through his body left William feeling nauseous.

After a few seconds had passed, George raised his head and looked at William. Two deep furrows had appeared across George's forehead. William looked into George's eyes and they seemed full of sadness. Seemingly lost for words, George just nodded ever so slightly to himself, before standing up and walking over towards the bedroom doorway. Coming to a standstill in the doorway, George turned around to face William.
"Oh, I had nearly forgotten to thank you for looking after Saba. I took care of her cut and she's already making a start on the eland enclosure. Why don't you wash yourself up and go to help her?"

In spite of all that had just occurred, William could just imagine the mood Saba would be in if he went to see her now. She would be waving her arms dramatically and accusing him of abandoning her in her hour of need, as well as questioning whether they should be friends anymore. William would feel guilty and offer to clean out the eland enclosure for her. *Would I ever be able to tell her about what I saw today? Or perhaps, she already knows? She would have heard the gunshot and, knowing Saba, she definitely would have asked what it was,* William thought to himself.

"William, I have known your father for many years." William's thoughts were interrupted by George, who was still standing in the doorway. "Deep down, he **is** a good man! You may not be able to see it now but, one day, you will understand that he is doing all this for **you**!" With that, George walked out of the bedroom.

Wiping his face dry with both of his hands, William exhaled heavily one more time. As he sat on the edge of his bed, George's final words kept ringing out in William's head. "*One day you will understand that he is doing all this for* ***you****!" How on earth can George expect me to feel happy about the fact that animals are dying – just for me?* William thought to himself. To William, there could be no justification for letting people shoot the animals that he had grown to care about, and certainly not for money! *Surely there must be another way!*

William slammed the duvet with his fists. Looking around the room, he hoped the answer would magically burst into his head. In the corner of his bedroom, William suddenly caught sight of a framed picture which had remained in the exact same position ever since he could remember. Inside the rough wooden frame was a faded black and white photograph of his father and late mother. Gingerly, William rose from his bed and wandered over to the corner of his bedroom. He carefully lifted the framed picture down from the shelf and smiled to himself as he looked at the image. Sitting next to one another on a bench, William's mother was wrapped in his father's embrace and the pair seemed to be almost bursting with happiness. William smiled at his mother's beaming eyes and wondered what she would have thought of what his father was doing. *Would she have been as angry as me to find out what he was doing? Or would she have supported my father, telling me that this was the way of the world they lived in?* William continued to stare at the picture, searching desperately for an answer.

Outside, a series of roars from some of the farm's lions suddenly broke out, momentarily disrupting William's thoughts. Listening to their groans, William realised that he could not just stand around in his bedroom searching fruitlessly for the answer. Instead, until he could figure out exactly how he was going to change the fortunes of the animals on the farm, he was going to get back out there and continue to care for the animals as he had always done.

Carefully placing the picture back down onto the shelf, William turned around to face the bedroom door. After taking a final deep breath, William strode out of his bedroom with purpose, knowing that he had to find a way to change the fate of the animals at Anga Farm.

CHAPTER FOURTEEN

For the rest of the day, William tirelessly worked to clean out as many enclosures as he could, re-filling water supplies and feeding the animals. After her initial tantrum, as William had predicted, Saba eventually returned to her mischievous self and it was not long before she was trying to throw the giraffes' hay over William's head, or trying to trip him up from behind! Normally, Saba's childish behaviour annoyed William, as it often got in the way of him completing his chores. However, after the drama and heartache of earlier on, he was just glad of the respite.

During the day, William had allowed himself a few moments to visit Matimba. As soon as he had entered the enclosure, William noticed that Matimba was being even more affectionate than usual. As odd as it seemed to William, he could not help but think that, somehow, Matimba knew how William was feeling inside. William had been able to hide it from Saba, but not from Matimba. Much to William's delight, Matimba rolled enthusiastically around his enclosure and repeatedly jumped up at William, licking his face with his rough tongue. Matimba even copied Saba's trick of trying to trip William up without being detected, using his large front paws whenever William was not looking!

Exhausted by Matimba's overly enthusiastic behaviour, William had sat down. However, it was not long before Matimba demanded some more attention off William, and the white lion padded over to brush his mane against William's legs, obviously asking for an intensive scratching session. After just a few moments of being lovingly scratched, Matimba became restless and decided that he wanted to play a new game. Carefully, the white lion began to shift his entire body on top of William, who fought back with all his strength. This was not the first time Matimba had tried to play this game with William, and the weight of an adolescent lion landing on top of a young boy meant that there was only ever one winner!

Matimba wriggled and repositioned himself until he had somehow managed to place his head into William's arms. William began to run his fingers through Matimba's mane and the white lion soon closed his eyes. It was not long before Matimba had fallen asleep and, aside from the lion's occasional grunting and groaning, the pair remained on the concrete floor in silence until it was time for William to return to his chores.

Since William had left his bedroom earlier that day, his father had purposefully been avoiding his son, always finding jobs to do which required him to be at the opposite end of the farm to where William was working. In fact, the only time William caught sight of his father that day was when his father was running across the courtyard towards the farmhouse to answer the phone, which had been unusually busy throughout the afternoon. William continued to work late into the evening until, eventually, he had completed all of his chores. If he was honest with himself, he too did not want to be near his father, so he purposefully took longer to complete his chores than usual. Just the thought of bumping into his father in the kitchen, or possibly having to pass him on the porch steps, made William's back stiffen up and the hairs on his arms stand on end.

As the sun was beginning to set, William wearily made his way from the giraffes' enclosure back towards the farmhouse. In the ever-fading light, William looked around to see if he could see his father. William finally made out the blurry silhouette of his father moving around inside the farm's store room. William wanted to seize this opportunity to get something to eat and go to bed, earlier than usual if necessary, before his father decided to turn in for the night as well.

After quickly walking up the porch steps, William quietly opened the back door and walked in, hoping not to attract his father's attention. Once in the kitchen, William walked over to the stove and ladled out a generous portion of butternut soup, which Saba's mother had prepared for William and his father earlier that week. William decided it was better to have it cold than to spend time heating it up and risk his father coming into the kitchen whilst it got warm. William quickly retreated to his bedroom and sat down on the edge of his bed. He planned to spend the rest of the evening sipping his soup and trying to come up with some kind of plan in order to persuade his father that there was a better way of making money from the farm. However, after just a couple of sips of his soup, William's eyes became heavy. William stretched out his legs and rested his head on top of his pillows. *I'll just close my eyes for a moment,* William decided.

It was not long before the day's events caught up with William. After initially fighting off his tiredness, William gave in and fell fast asleep in his overalls.

CHAPTER FIFTEEN

The next morning, William woke up wearily. It took several moments before his vision adjusted to the blinding light which was beaming in through his bedroom window. William looked down and realised that he was still wearing his overalls from yesterday. As he eventually found the strength to lift himself off the bed, William's right foot clumsily knocked over the bowl of half-eaten soup from the night before, causing the contents to spill out all over the wooden floor.

"Oh you've got to be joking!" William muttered to himself in annoyance. *I'll clean it later* he quickly decided. William was too eager to go and see Matimba to start cleaning the floor now. Still not fully awake, he ventured sluggishly out of his bedroom and quickly looked around the farmhouse. His father was nowhere to be seen. Apart from the faintest sounds coming from the animals outside, an eerie stillness loomed over the farmhouse, and little dust particles appeared to be hanging unnaturally in the air, catching the sunlight. Unfazed by the peculiar atmosphere, William yawned one more time and made his way into the kitchen. Relieved at the thought of being on his own, William grabbed two pieces of bread from a loaf which his father must have left out earlier that morning and spread both with a thick coat of butter and fruit jam. William then picked up a relatively clean mug from next to the sink and filled it up with cold water. It was not long before William had wolfed down all of his breakfast, and was making his way out of the back door and onto the porch.

Immediately, William was blinded by the sunlight which seemed to be beaming down on him stronger than ever. He quickly placed his right hand over his eyes to shield himself from the glare which was reflecting off every surface close to him. William's eyes soon adjusted and he looked around the farm, trying to locate his father. To his right, lions were clambering over one another in their enclosures, selfishly trying to find even the smallest patch of shade in which to cool down. To his left, The Twins had both sought refuge from the heat under their feeding platform. William smiled at the pair. Try as they might, both of them were far too tall to fit their entire bodies under the platform. As a result, the giraffes had to keep turning around to give both their heads and their rears a turn under the platform!

As William began to make his way towards the main lion enclosures, he caught sight of his father, kneeling over a water trough outside of Matimba's enclosure. He was scrubbing it furiously with a small brush in his right hand. William was used to this scene. The water troughs had to be cleaned regularly to stop the animals on the farm from catching infections from any stale water which had been left out in the heat for too long. The only way to clean the troughs without constant interruptions from a young lion was to clean them outside the enclosure.

William used to think that his father did strenuous work like this out of love but, today, William looked at it differently. Today, William saw his father's actions through a new pair of eyes. With each step, William could feel the anger in the pit of his stomach rising. All the hard work his father had carried out had purely been to keep the animals alive so somebody could come to their farm and shoot them! William shook his head in anger. He had to do something! Suddenly, William thought that he must try to change his father's mind. *Maybe, just maybe, if he could see how much I care for Matimba, then he might change his mind.* William had to try at least!

"Glad to see you've gotten over your little temper tantrum!" William's father began before his son could speak, not bothering to even look up from the arduous job. "I need your help today!" The malicious tone in his father's voice took William aback. Once again, William's back stiffened and the hairs on his arms stood on end. William struggled to think of something to say back to his father. In the silence and, still without even looking up to acknowledge his son, William's father stopped scrubbing the trough and picked up a metal bucket, filled to the brim with crystal clear water. He rinsed away the soap which had covered the majority of the trough, and carried on as though William was not even there.
"Well have you? Or are you still going to make a big deal out of it?" William's father was now becoming irritated by his son's lack of response. His father's irritable mood made it even harder for William to choose even a single word, and William continued to fumble for something to say. William's father had now placed the empty bucket behind him, and

carried on scrubbing the edges of the trough. Compared to the hundreds of times that William had watched his father carry out this simple chore, he had never seen his father do it so aggressively. Every scrub appeared like a vicious blow. His father was scowling at the trough. His brow was drenched with sweat. His face burned and the veins on his neck seemed to be trying to burst out. William was genuinely frightened by his father's behaviour, so he looked into Matimba's enclosure for some comfort.

William looked towards every corner, but he could not see his friend. Assuming that Matimba was probably sleeping in his birthing den, William took a few steps closer. However, as he neared, he realised that Matimba was nowhere to be seen. *Where is he?* William quickly checked again in every corner of the enclosure. Matimba was not there! He looked again at the birthing den. Nothing! Panic stricken, William turned around. Before he could ask anything, William noticed a thick metal chain glistening in the grass. As he followed the chain with his eyes, William's heart began to race as he instantly recognised the brown, leather collar! It was the same brown, leather collar which his father had used almost two years ago to move the pregnant Bahiya to this very enclosure.
"Where is he?" William shrieked at his father. "Where is Matimba?"

William had never shouted at his father before in his entire life. He had always been too frightened to. But this was different! Instead of answering, his father simply continued to scrub the trough, as if his son had said nothing.
"Where is he?" William yelled again.
Without answering his son's question, William's father carried

on scrubbing - the trough was now shinier than when it was new!
"Well, you're going to have to get used to it because I've finally set a date for him." William's father nodded towards the empty enclosure where Matimba should have been, but still continued with his chore.

What? William was lost for words. *What did he mean, "I've finally set a date for him?"* Then it dawned on William what his father had done. As his father rinsed the trough one more time, his words stirred in William's mind like a terrible dream. William tried as hard as he could not to imagine it!
"No!" William exclaimed under his breath as he shook his head and closed his eyes as tight as he could, trying his upmost to rid his mind of the thought. But, try as he might, William saw it in his mind. William saw what his father had set "a date" for. Instead of the Big Fella, William's mind pictured Matimba's bullet-ridden body squirming in the air in pain.
"No!" William said again, tears now rolling down both of his cheeks. "Please, no!" he yelled. William covered his eyes, trying to block the same sequence of events from replaying again and again in his mind.

"I knew it!" William's father's voice suddenly woke William from the nightmare vision. William gasped aloud, struggling to breathe after what he had just witnessed in his mind.
"I knew I shouldn't have trusted you to raise that lion! You've become way too attached!" William's father was now standing in front of his son, looking at him with disgust. "I just regret not doing this earlier." William's father bellowed as he threw the brush at the trough below him in frustration.

"The time has come for him to do something for us for a change. A regular client of mine is in the area. The client used to beg me to get hold of a white lion for them. It's the only reason they began hunting so they could net a white one. The client is willing to pay way over the asking price to fulfil their dream. Enough to keep us fed for years to come! That is why Matimba was always more important than the rest of the animals on this farm!"

William's father knelt down and picked up the metal chain, wrapping it tightly around his fist, before grasping the brown leather collar with his other hand. Towering back to his feet, he turned away without even looking at William and began to make his way across the courtyard towards the store and food-preparation building. After only a few strides, William's father stopped and turned to face his son.
"They'll be here tomorrow."

In a complete state of shock, William watched his father leave without saying a single word. William wanted to scream and shout at his father, to tell him how much he hated him for the pain he was causing his own son! At the same time, William wanted to cry out loud and beg him to change his mind. However, nothing came out of his mouth. Instead, William fell to his knees and cried. Holding his head in his hands, tears poured from William's eyes and he sobbed uncontrollably. *How could he do this to me? How could my own father take away the most important thing in my life?*

Suddenly, William heard footsteps. Looking up from his hands, William could just make out the blurred frame of George, standing only a few metres away. George must have heard everything and now seemed to be watching William's father as he walked across the courtyard. George shook his head, seemingly in disbelief, and then exploded into a sprint. Running at a frantic pace, it was only a matter of seconds before George had stormed up onto the porch, through the back door and out of sight into the farmhouse.

CHAPTER SIXTEEN

Kneeling on the dusty path which ran alongside the perimeter of the paddock, William stroked Matimba's ever-growing mane through the enclosure's steel fencing. Since his father's revelation, William had spent the entire afternoon with Matimba, neglecting his duties on the farm so he could be with his friend. Unconcerned at abandoning his chores, William knew he had to spend every available second with Matimba until he could figure out a solution to this madness! William would have joined his friend inside the paddock, had his father not padlocked the enclosure door shut.

Despite what had transpired over the last few hours, Anga Farm appeared no different. In the distance, William could just make out the heads of the farm's twin giraffes as they munched happily on the hay on the platform in their enclosure. To William's left, the hyenas were chasing around after each other, every so often letting out a high pitched shriek. When they caught one another, the more dominant would bite the other on the ear - a tactic which George had told William the hyenas used to assert their dominance. In the sky above, birds which William could never remember the names of soared on a gentle breeze in the bright blue sky.

William turned back and smiled at Matimba who was blissfully sleeping alongside the paddock's perimeter fencing. With his back to William, Matimba was completely unaware of the threat he was facing. Even in the late afternoon, with the sun beginning to fade, the lion's white fur still glowed with magnificence. William could not understand how anybody could ever want to harm something so magical and beautiful!

Sitting cross-legged up against the paddock's fencing, William shook his head in frustration. He just could not understand why this was happening or, more importantly, how he was meant to stop it.
"There must be a way!" he muttered aloud, pulling up a few shoots of grass at the same time in annoyance.

"George! Where are you?" William's father barked from somewhere in the middle of the farm's courtyard, out of William's view.
"George!" Once again, William's father called out but, this time, he sounded far more irritated. William listened for a response whilst still stroking Matimba's mane, but there was nothing. William had not seen George since he had watched him running into the farmhouse earlier that day. Despite the state that William had been in at the time, he had found George's hastiness very strange and unusual. For as long as William had known George, he had never seen him behave like that. *Where had he gone? Why was he in such a rush? How much of my father's conversation with me had George heard?* William did

not know the answer to any of these questions, but George had not yet returned and it was obvious that his father did not know where George was either.

William got to his feet and rubbed the grass and dirt off his knees. As William turned around and looked at all of the other enclosures on the farm, he suddenly felt guilty. It was not fair to all the other animals if he just sat outside Matimba's enclosure all day. Whatever his father had done or was going to do, it was not their fault and there was no way his father could give them the care they required all by himself. Reluctantly, William decided that he should, just for a little while, leave Matimba alone in his enclosure and clean out some of the grazers' enclosures at least.
"I will be back as soon as I can! I promise!" William reassuringly whispered through the perimeter fence towards his friend. William received no reply as Matimba was fast asleep! William crept away from the paddock and made his way over to the food preparation room.

As William approached, he began to hear an unusual humming noise in the distance. Not giving it much thought, William continued on his way. However, the peculiar humming sound seemed to get louder and louder with every step William took. William realised that the noise was coming from ahead of him, in the same direction as the farmhouse. Then, all of a sudden, the mysterious noise stopped. In the silence, William held his breath in anticipation. Now only a few metres away from the food-preparation building, William listened closely to see if and when the strange humming would start again.

"Creeeek!" Another unexpected noise momentarily caught William off guard. In shock, his entire body shuddered but, despite being unexpected, William recognised this sound. It was the farm's gate being opened. William assumed that George must be back. *But what was the humming sound?* William asked himself.

Out of nowhere, an engine roared into action! To William's immediate left, the farm's three hyenas retreated in fear, searching for the nearest available cover. Immediately, William realised that the strange humming he had heard before must have been from some sort of motorised vehicle driving up the main track towards the farm. "George doesn't have a car!" William suddenly whispered to himself. Desperate to know who it was and why they were there, William crept along the edge of the food preparation room. Suddenly, a white jeep raced across the farm's courtyard before skidding to a halt right in front of the farmhouse porch, leaving in its wake a cloud of dust. Looking at the jeep, William decided that it was time to investigate who was in the vehicle and what they wanted.

William set off across the courtyard, keeping low so as not to attract the attention of the visitors or his father. Ahead of him, the jeep remained stationary, showing no sign of life whatsoever. William edged closer and closer towards the vehicle, still remaining low to the ground. Finally, he reached the jeep and hid around the back.

All of a sudden, the jeep's two front doors swung open. Out of the passenger side, a blond haired woman jumped energetically out of the vehicle. Wearing khaki shorts and a royal blue t-shirt, the woman looked youthful in her movements as she shut the door firmly behind her. Transfixed, William watched her every move until she disappeared entirely from view around the front of the vehicle. William had been so captivated by the attractiveness of the woman that he had not noticed who the other person getting out of the jeep was. Then, suddenly, William panicked. *What if they need something from out of the boot?* Without giving it a second thought, he quietly edged back around the side of the jeep, his heart pounding in his chest.

As he moved, William was able to inspect the side of the jeep once more, and a logo stopped William in his tracks! Above the black outline of a male lion, printed in a thick blue typeface, the logo read *'Lion Rescue Foundation!'* Staggered, William read it back once again. Taking his time, he processed every letter carefully.

William suddenly felt a rush of excitement. *Did they know about Matimba? Were they here to save him?* William felt exhilarated at the thought. After the last few hours of despair, William finally had a glimmer of hope! Struggling to contain his excitement, William crept purposefully back towards the rear of the jeep, his face beaming with anticipation. William had to see who it was and what they were going to do to save Matimba! However, as William peered around the corner of the vehicle to get a better view, he was shocked to see George standing beside the two strangers, all with their backs turned to William.

"Bang!" The ear-splitting sound of the farm's kitchen door being slammed open made the two strangers, George and

William jump in fear. William's entire body shuddered as he looked up at the porch. Standing in the empty doorway, William's father glared down at the trio with his fists clenched.

"What are **you** doing here again?" William's father roared down at the trio. William's back stiffened and, anxiously, he looked back towards George and the two strangers.
"Enough is enough, Michael!" George exclaimed as he took a few steps towards William's father. William had never heard George speak so aggressively before, and certainly not towards his father.

"George, what are you doing?" Shocked, William's father seemed completely taken aback by what George had said.
"Spare the white lion and stop all this madness, Michael!" William's entire body tensed up at the mere mention of Matimba. *Was George going to save Matimba?* Excited at the thought, William's heart began to race.
"Consider what you are doing, my friend!" George pleaded. "It doesn't have to be this way! You can make a difference, a real difference. You can save the white lion, and all the other animals on the farm!" William couldn't believe what he was hearing! He closed his eyes and prayed that his father would listen. Looking back at the porch, William noticed that George had walked up one of the steps towards William's father.

"You are a good man, Michael!" The porch steps creaked as George continued up another. "You are just trying to do the best for William!" William gasped involuntarily when George mentioned his name. Immediately, he threw his right hand over his mouth and his cheeks turned red, hoping nobody had heard him. Holding his breath, William dared not even move a single muscle!

"So…*this* is how you repay me, bro?" The response from William's father reassured William that he had not been discovered. On the other hand, William immediately felt sick! He knew from the tone in his father's voice that he would not listen to George's plea. William looked back around the rear of the jeep and saw his father stepping towards George, pointing straight at him.
"You have betrayed me, George!" William's father whispered accusingly.
"No, my friend, that is not my…" George tried to explain.
"I don't want to hear it!" William's father bellowed. The force of his words caused William's entire body to flinch!
"I thought I could trust you, George…but I was obviously wrong! I want you and your lion-hugging friends to get out of here! I **never** want to see you again!" The malice in his father's words terrified William! They left George with no doubt that he would never be allowed to visit the farm again. *But what about Saba?* Two tears trailed slowly down William's cheeks, as he suddenly realised that his father was not only taking Matimba away from him, but also Saba. The deafening sound of the kitchen door being slammed shut caused William to shudder once again and he looked back around the rear of the jeep towards the trio.

The three looked at one another in silence. The stillness seemed to last for an age as William waited for one of the three to say something, something which might give him a glimmer of hope.

"We have failed!" The mystery blonde woman broke the silence. In her trembling voice, William could hear and feel the same desperation and anguish which he too was riddled with.
"No!" The defiance in George's voice startled William. "We must not give up!"

All of a sudden, William heard the shuffling of feet moving across the front of the jeep. Looking underneath the vehicle, William could see three pairs of feet, one to his left and two to his right. Both of the jeep's doors swung open and the trio quickly jumped in. A thunderous growl from the jeep's engine blasted out from the exhaust pipe, causing William to cry out with fright! William covered his ears with both of his hands and he kept his eyes firmly fixed on the jeep as it roared noisily away, smothering him in a plume of dust. As the cloud settled, the deep humming of the jeep's engine grew fainter and fainter as it moved further and further away from the farm. William stood up and removed his hands from his ears. He patted away the dirt which had covered him and George's final words rang out inside his ears. "We must not give up! We must not give up!" Looking back towards the paddock, William's heart warmed and he smiled to himself. Finally, there was some hope to hold onto!

CHAPTER SEVENTEEN

As the sun began to disappear behind the distant mountains, William had just completed the last of his daily chores - restocking the hay, acacia leaves and carrots on the giraffes' feeding platform. With the farm now shrouded in darkness, William settled down alongside the perimeter fence of the paddock, watching Matimba wander aimlessly through his new living area, occasionally stopping to rub his face against the thick bushes which were scattered around inside the enclosure.

Like all lions on the farm, Matimba became more active at night. Since Matimba had been moved out of the farmhouse and into one of the smaller enclosures, William only ever seemed to watch the white lion sleep. The only time William really saw Matimba become animated was during feeding time, or when he awoke from a deep sleep to have a quick drink. Watching Matimba restlessly move around his new enclosure, inspecting every single new sight and smell, William felt like he was seeing a new side of the white lion.

Without warning, the familiar sound of an American entertainer, singing theatrically, rang out from within the farmhouse, causing William to spin around. The singing was accompanied by a crackling piano tune, which made the record sound even older than it probably was. Every so often, after a long day working on the farm, William's father would relax by listening to records on his antique vinyl player. In front of the paddock, William could imagine his father, sitting in his favourite chair with his eyes closed, humming along to the words and tapping his fingers on the edge of the chair's arm-rest. William's father always listened to American singers as he maintained that they were the best. William could never remember their names, despite his father's encouragement, and this was probably because he did not like vinyl music much. It was too loud for William and he never understood why anyone would want to listen to that when they could listen to the sounds on the farm.

Ignoring the racket, William looked back at Matimba. At that moment, it suddenly dawned on William that this could be the last few moments that he got to spend with his best friend. Whilst Matimba inspected yet another branch from an overgrown bush, William thought about his father, sat in his chair in the farmhouse, listening to music.

If he would just listen to me. If he just knew how much I love Matimba then he might change his mind. William watched Matimba sniffing a small bunch of leaves on a branch, and he knew that he could not give up so easily.

"I've got to try again!" Matimba suddenly stopped still at the sound of William's voice. A part of William knew that it probably would not work, but he had to try! For just a moment, William thought back to George's words, "We must not give up!" William had no idea what George was planning to do and when he was planning to do it. William could not help but feel that, by doing nothing and simply relying on George, he was gambling Matimba's life on a hope - a hope that George would return to save the white lion before it was too late! Clambering back to his feet, William knew he had to try one final time to convince his father to change his mind!

William crossed the courtyard with purpose. In front of him, the farmhouse had almost disappeared from view, cloaked by the darkness. In fact, only the kitchen's flickering light bulb, barely visible through the small kitchen window, guided William towards the porch. Above William's head, a small flock of birds called out to one another as they flew across the night sky. William walked quietly up the porch steps and stared up at the birds. Flying off into the distance, the small flock could barely be seen against the night sky. Only their calls gave their presence away. William wondered what the farm would be like when they returned. *Would the flock of birds look down as they flew by to see a white lion wandering around his enclosure? Or would they just see an empty one?* Filled with determination at the thought of losing Matimba, William opened the back door and walked into the kitchen, convinced that what he was doing was right. He had to continue to fight for the life of his best friend!

Instantly, William was hit by a wall of sound. The music was far louder in the farmhouse than it had sounded from outside. It made William's fingers tingle and the ends of his toes vibrate. However, William was used to this. Ever since he was a young boy, his father had always loved playing his music loudly!

But suddenly, everything went quiet! In the shadow-filled house, the silence felt eerie, almost scary. William could feel the tips of his fingers continuing to gently tingle. In the stillness, every one of William's breaths sounded even louder than they actually were. He tiptoed as lightly as he could through the kitchen, trying not to make a single sound. William looked at the wooden kitchen table in the middle of the room. On it, he noticed several empty green beer bottles. Looking forwards once again, William continued to creep through the kitchen. Despite his best attempts, every floorboard he stood on seemed to groan. At any second, William expected his father to burst into the kitchen to berate his son for interrupting his music. However, his father never appeared. Instead, William continued to tiptoe through the kitchen, towards the sitting room.

The flickering light from the kitchen bulb intermittently lit up the sitting room and, as William peered in from the kitchen, he saw his father sitting in his favourite chair. On the floor, to the right of the chair, William spied two more empty green beer bottles. These were led on their sides underneath a small wooden table which the antique vinyl player sat on top of. However, the vinyl record was no longer spinning and the turntable needle had been lifted up. It was at that moment that William immediately knew that his father must have heard him! In spite of this, his father still said nothing. He just remained still in his chair. In the eerie silence, William suddenly remembered Matimba, wandering back and forth in the paddock, and what would happen to the white lion if he did or said nothing. William knew that he could no longer remain silent!

"Please don't let Matimba die," William uttered. "I am begging you!" William's words were spoken softly yet, in the silence, he knew that his father would hear him. Seconds passed by and William's father still said nothing. William knew that his father was probably still furious with him, but the least he could do was answer his son's plea.
"Please," William pleaded. "Please. He is my best friend and I will be lost without him. I know that if Mum was still alive…"

William's father suddenly rose to his feet! In doing so, he knocked over the wooden table next to his chair, causing the antique vinyl player to come crashing down onto the floor. The two glass bottles rolled across the floor in opposite directions.
"How dare you use your mother against me!" William's father bellowed at his son. He flew at William and grabbed him by the collar. The force of the grasp knocked William backwards, and he nearly fell to the ground. William's father leant into his son and screamed, "You're no son of mine!" The power of his father's words blew William's hair back, and tears began to run down his face.

Still holding onto William's collar, William's father dragged his son across the sitting room and towards his bedroom. William struggled to get to his feet as his father continued to drag him. His knees kept banging against the hard floor and William was crying out in pain. Undeterred, William's father continued to drag his frightened son towards the bedroom.

"*Bang!*" William's father kicked the bedroom door wide open with a single swipe of his right foot. Without any hesitation, he dragged William through the doorway and forcefully threw him onto the bed.

"You're no son of mine!" he screamed once again at his son before storming off and violently slamming the bedroom door shut behind him.

CHAPTER EIGHTEEN

In the darkness, all alone, William sat on the edge of his bed. Since his father's outburst, William had barely moved; too terrified to even check over the areas of his body that ached. William's hands shook so violently that they struggled to even grasp his duvet properly. Tears rolled down William's cheeks as he struggled to catch his breath, too frightened to exhale loudly in case his father heard him. Although it had been several minutes since his father had slammed shut the bedroom door, the hairs on William's arms still stood on end and cold shudders continued to run repeatedly throughout his body. William knew that he could no longer rely on his father to do the right thing. Foolishly, William had put his faith in his father. William knew that if he was going to help save Matimba, he was going to have to rely on others.

Suddenly, he had an idea! He sat up straight and let go of his duvet. His knees were sore, but William no longer cared. The tears in his eyes cleared and the cold shudders disappeared. William knew that he had to find the only person who could help him. That person was George!

William was sure that he could remember his way to George's house. He had been there several times before. The thought of George reminded William of the raft of lies that his father and George had fed to him for years. But William did not have time for that. He had to save Matimba and time was running out! Shaking away his anger, William hatched a plan! He knew that there was no way he could sneak out whilst his father was still awake. He looked up at the clock on the shelf, next to the portrait of his mother and father. It read 21:23. William's body began to warm as his plan suddenly came together. William was determined that he was going to do something to help save Matimba. He would not fail! He could not fail!

William planned to wait a few more hours, probably two or three, until he was sure that his father had fallen fast asleep. Then, without his father knowing, he would sneak out of the house and run as fast as he could down the main track towards George's house. There, William would be safe and he could help George come up with a plan to save Matimba. The thought made William sit up straight with excitement. His father's outburst was now a distant thought, William had more important things to worry about!

William lay back on his bed and rested his head against a pillow. Again and again he plotted the route to George's house. Again and again he was certain that he knew it. *Sure, it will be dark and yes, it might be dangerous,* William thought, *but I have to try!* As William went over the route again and again, he gently closed his eyes. He pictured each stage of the journey in his mind, eager to save Matimba from his terrible fate in the morning!

CHAPTER NINETEEN

William squinted as he struggled to fully open his eyes. Every time he tried, a bright, blinding light caused them to immediately close.
"Aahh!" William yawned loudly, as he stretched out his arms and legs on the bed.

Then, immediately, William sat up in horror! He had fallen asleep! *No! I couldn't have!* William looked over at his clock. It read 10:00!

"I'm such an idiot!" William yelled at himself. In a state of panic, he jumped up from his bed and ran over to the bedroom door. Grabbing the door knob, he quickly tried to open it. However, every time he tried turning it, nothing happened. Again and again, William turned the door knob in every direction possible, but his door still would not open! Then it dawned on him - his father must have locked it whilst he was asleep! His father must have known that William was going to try and do something to save Matimba! William's mind raced furiously.

"I need to get out of this room!" William screamed out loud as he kicked the bedroom door out of frustration. He tried again and again to open the door and, the more he failed, the more incensed he became! William frantically pulled, pushed and shook the door knob, but to no avail. In desperation, William put his ear up against the door and listened carefully, trying to hear if anyone was outside. William could just make out a strange, muffled sound. *Was that somebody talking?* He pushed his ear even harder up against the bedroom door, oblivious to the pain that it caused, desperate to hear more! But the sound quickly faded away.

"No!" William punched the door with his fists this time, ignoring the shearing pain which erupted in his right hand. "Let me out!" Without any time to lose, William looked around him and remembered his bedroom window. William knew that his father had lost the key to it many years ago and had never bothered to replace it. But even though William knew that his bedroom window could not be opened, he had to try! He had to get out of his bedroom! In a state of frenzy, he darted over to the window and, with all his strength, he tried to lift up the bottom part of the window. William pushed and pulled with every last ounce of strength remaining in his body, but it still would not budge!

Taking a step back, he wiped the sweat from his brow and tried to think of something else. Without hesitation, William searched his bedroom for something to smash the window with. Then it came to him - the clock! Spinning around, William dashed over to the shelf and grabbed the clock! He carefully took a few steps backwards to allow himself a short run up. William had no idea how he was going to get rid of the remaining glass that would be left in the window, or how on earth he was going to fit through the gap, but he knew that he had to try something! Readying himself to throw as hard as he could, William pulled his arm back.

Out of nowhere, William heard the roaring sound of an engine! At first, he could barely make it out. Yet, with every second that passed, it got louder and louder as it got closer to the farmhouse! *Was it the hunter arriving to shoot Matimba?* With his right fist still grasping the clock, William listened carefully. He threw his ear up against the door but the sound had now stopped! Seconds passed by but he heard absolutely nothing!
"No!" William cried out loud as he slammed his left hand against the bedroom door. "Let me out!" Turning around, William ran at the window as fast as he could and threw his clock with every bit of strength that he could muster!

"*Crash!*" The clock smashed through the top right side of the window pane, causing several shards of glass to soar into the air! William looked up at the hole he had made. His stomach sank as he knew that there was no chance he would ever make it through such a small gap. William needed something bigger and he needed it fast! Outside his bedroom, William suddenly heard raised voices! "I'm running out of time!" William screamed out loud. Frantically, he looked around his room for something big.

"*Click, click.*" Within an instant, William froze.
"What was that?" he whispered to himself.
"*Click, click…click, click, click.*" William heard the strange noise again coming from behind him.
"*Click, click…click, click, click.*" William took a step closer to

his bedroom door.
"Click, click…click, click, click." William felt a sudden surge of excitement as he realised that it was someone fiddling with the bedroom door lock. Before he could do or say anything, the bedroom door burst open! There, standing in the doorway, was Saba!

"Come on, we haven't got much time! They're already here!" Saba shouted! Without saying a single word, William bolted passed Saba, through the farmhouse and out of the back door. The first thing that William noticed was a white jeep, which he immediately recognised from the day before. It was parked just a few metres away from the porch and two of its doors had been left open. On the passenger door, William noticed the same logo of a male lion, with the heading *'Lion Rescue Foundation!'* written above it in blue. William then heard raised voices!

Straight ahead and across the courtyard, William saw the same blond woman from the day before, standing next to George and William's father. All three were shouting and pointing aggressively at one another. William knew that this was his chance! With his father distracted, he could open the paddock door and release Matimba. Without giving it a second thought, William burst into action! He cleared the porch steps with a single leap and sprinted as fast as he could across the courtyard, heading towards the paddock. William could hear Saba's footsteps behind him but, try as she might, there was no way she could keep up with him. William did not have time to wait for her to catch up - he had to save Matimba!

Within a matter of seconds, he had reached the food preparation room. Without even looking to see if he had been spotted by his father, George or the blond woman, William sprinted around the side of the room. Then immediately, he came to a standstill. Standing in the middle of the paddock, a tall woman with an enormous rifle was creeping forwards behind a thick bush. From where he was stood, William could just make out that the woman was wearing a dark green, brimmed hat, with her black hair tied up underneath it. She was dressed from head to toe in camouflage gear and wore a large pair of dark sun glasses.

William followed the direction that she was moving in with his eyes. She was heading straight towards Matimba! To make matters even worse, Matimba was heading straight towards the woman! With his head and shoulders low to the ground, the white lion's eyes were firmly fixed on the unfamiliar woman in front of him. Curiosity was getting the better of him and he continued to creep closer and closer towards her.

Panic stricken, William dashed over towards the paddock door and, with every last bit of strength left in his body, he threw it open! Without thinking, William sprinted straight towards the woman, running as fast as his body would allow. The woman silently raised her rifle, and took aim at Matimba. The white lion recoiled at her sudden movements and let out a loud roar.

"William! No!" William's father's voice rang out.

Suddenly, a loud gunshot exploded around the farm!

CHAPTER TWENTY

All of a sudden, Matimba woke up. Looking around in every direction, the white lion soon realised that he was all alone. The large acacia tree which loomed over him provided a welcome patch of shade as the white lion took another look around, checking for any signs of danger. Matimba shook his head, trying to help his eyes become more accustomed to the blinding sunlight. It was then that he smelt it! Somewhere ahead of him, there was food! He could not see it - the sunlight was too bright - but he knew it was out there!

Immediately, Matimba decided that he had to go in search of this food! He tried to lift himself up but, for some reason, he could not manage it! Over and over again, Matimba tried to get to his feet but, with each attempt, he would suddenly collapse back down to the ground. This had never happened to Matimba before and he did not know what to do! He desperately needed to eat! Pushing harder than he had ever pushed before, the white lion finally managed to heave himself up off the ground.

Matimba was now standing up on all fours, but he knew that something was not right. For some unknown reason, Matimba rocked uncontrollably from side to side, and he felt as if he could crash back down into a heap again at any moment. However, after a few seconds had passed by, Matimba gradually felt the strength in each of his legs start to come back. The white lion gently placed a single paw out in front of him. Despite a slight wobble, Matimba attempted it again with another paw. This time, he felt even more comfortable. He then tried another paw, then another. The more steps he took the more he could smell food!

"*Click!*" Suddenly, Matimba froze! He looked over to his left towards where the strange noise had come from. Looking closely, Matimba saw something which he had never seen before! It was dark and extremely large. The white lion continued to glare at the object which was moving slowly, unsure about whether it posed a threat or not. Matimba had recently learned that unfamiliar looking things were often dangerous and it was best to avoid them whenever possible. Despite this, his empty stomach was desperate for food. Driven by hunger, Matimba decided to continue on.

In the four wheel drive safari truck, Saba turned her camera lens to zoom in on Matimba. Peering through the view-finder, she focussed in on Matimba whilst he ravenously feasted on the meat between his front paws. With a click of her right finger, she took another photograph of the white lion. This was the first meal Matimba was enjoying in his new home, and Saba desperately wanted to capture every single moment of it! As she pulled the camera away from her eye, a single tear rolled down her cheek and dropped onto her lap.

"He would have loved to have seen this." Saba whispered out loud, her voice quivering with emotion.
"Yes, he certainly would." George agreed. "This would have made him very happy indeed." Standing beside Saba, George placed a supportive arm around his daughter as the pair watched Matimba in the distance. Occasionally, the white lion would glance back up at the truck, obviously still unsure about its presence.

As George and Saba continued to speak to one another, William's father remained silent. He knew that if his son had been there, he would have cherished the moment forever. All that William ever wanted was to give Matimba more space in which to roam and to, one day, see him living alongside other lions.

As William's father took in a deep breath to try and compose himself, he also knew that his son would have been delighted to know that, instead of carrying on with his hunting business, Anga Farm was now running as a successful sanctuary for ex-captive or injured animals, allowing them to live out the rest of their lives with some dignity. Following the wishes of William's father and with the support of several of the local tribes, Matimba and several of the other lions at Anga Farm had been moved, under anaesthetic, to a remote reserve several miles south of Anga. Matimba's new home was entirely fenced off from the outside world, yet included a few prey species which, over time, it was hoped he would eventually start to stalk and chase!

Matimba would never be a free roaming wild lion - he was too reliant on people for food and he had not been taught any of the necessary skills that he would need to become a successful hunter or to socially interact with other lions. Despite this, as William's father watched Matimba feeding enthusiastically on the meat beneath him, he thought back to what Saba and George had just said. He knew they were right - if William was sat with them today, he would have been proud of how his father had changed!

With that thought in his mind, William's father turned the key in the truck's ignition, and the engine roared into life. Taking one more look at Matimba, William's father smiled to himself and placed his foot gently onto the accelerator.
"It's time to go," he whispered.

AFTERWORD BY LIONAID

The lion captive breeding industry to supply the trophy hunting trade in South Africa has grown into a highly lucrative commercial enterprise over the past five years. It is also an immoral, unethical and sordid practice that has significantly stained South Africa's conservation image.

The more details that emerge about this industry, the more the world public and indeed South African citizens are expressing their disgust that this kind of crass commercialism has been allowed to develop in a nation that attempts to identify itself as a leader in African wildlife conservation. Over the five years 2007-2011, South Africa exported 4,090 lion trophies, virtually all derived from captive bred lion hunts.

The demand for more and more trophies has led to the establishment of additional lion captive breeding programmes in Namibia, Botswana, Zimbabwe and Zambia.

LionAid, September 2013

LionAid is a small but highly effective charity, based in the UK, focused mainly but not exclusively on reversing the catastrophic declines in lion populations, caused by loss of habitat and prey, human/wildlife conflict, trophy hunting, trade in lion bone and lion body parts and cub smuggling for the pet and canned hunting trade.

LionAid believes that there are now only five viable lion populations left in Africa and one small population in India.

For further information and to donate to their work, please visit their website: www.lionaid.org.

Made in the USA
Charleston, SC
10 September 2015